"I would keep you safe, Leonor. Protect you from all that is evil and dangerous."

"You know you cannot, Rey. You cannot be with me always. I must learn to protect myself. In your eyes I see two things— anguish and hunger. You are scarred, Rey. You must find some joy in this world to soften your distress."

Reynaud hesitated. Aye, he had discovered joy. Being near her, hearing her voice, admiring her wit, her courage. Even her stubbornness. Watching her sing those exquisite melodies that caught at his heart and ensnared his soul.

Wanting her.

* * *

Templar Knight, Forbidden Bride
Harlequin® Historical #914—September 2008

Author Note

In the late twelfth century southern France, or Languedoc as it was known then—long a breeding ground for heretics such as the Cathars—was sought by the Templars as a foothold for establishing a Templar presence. They owed allegiance to the pope, not the king of France; the kingdom of France wished not only to gain control of lands in southern France but to promote a crusade against Moorish Spain and drive out the Muslims who had ruled there since the eighth century.

Twelfth-century society in Moorish Spain was a rich mixture of Muslims, Arabized Christians known as Mozarabs, and Jews. The Knights of Solomon's Temple, or Knights Templar, founded in 1118 AD, was the most respected military order of the time, trusted and admired by both crusaders and Saracens. The rival Order of St. John, or Hospitalers, never gained either the reputation or the enormous treasury garnered by the Templars, who served as bankers as well as diplomatic emissaries for both Muslims and Christians.

Southern France exhibited all the panache of the high Middle Ages: troubadours and the concept of courtly love; knights and ladies; tournaments and the code of chivalry; literary and cultural traditions that would be passed on into the Renaissance. Immortalized in songs and stories, it is an age we still relish.

TEMPLAR KNIGHT, FORBIDDEN BRIDE

Lynna Banning

HARLEQUIN®

TORONTO • NEW YORK • LONDON
AMSTERDAM • PARIS • SYDNEY • HAMBURG
STOCKHOLM • ATHENS • TOKYO • MILAN • MADRID
PRAGUE • WARSAW • BUDAPEST • AUCKLAND

ISBN-13: 978-0-373-29514-2
ISBN-10:   0-373-29514-6

TEMPLAR KNIGHT, FORBIDDEN BRIDE

Printed in U.S.A.

For my superb agent, Pattie Steele-Perkins.

With grateful thanks to Suzanne Barrett, Tricia Adams,
Kathleen Dougherty, Shirley Marcus, Brenda Preston,
Joan Powell, Norma Pulle, Dave Woolston and
Alicia Rasley.

Praise for Lynna Banning

Crusader's Lady

"Marc and Soraya's love story is touching, and the
plot will make you wonder until the last page how
they will get together."
—*Romantic Times BOOKreviews*

Loner's Lady

"Poignant tale of a woman's coming of age…"
—*Romantic Times BOOKreviews*

The Ranger and the Redhead

"Fast-paced, adventure-filled story."
—*Romantic Times BOOKreviews*

The Wedding Cake War

"You'll love Banning's subtle magic with romance."
—*Romantic Times BOOKreviews*

Chapter One

Emirate of Granada, 1167

Reynaud brought his warhorse to a halt and leaned his weary body forwards, scanning the rocky hillside overlooking the River Darro. Below him spread the muddle of flat-roofed houses and open courtyards that made up the Moorish quarter of the city. After twenty years, everything looked smaller than he remembered. He gazed down at the orange groves and almond orchards surrounding the towering stone walls, the whitewashed adobe buildings gleaming in the harsh afternoon sunlight, and felt his gut tighten.

He was home.

He clenched his teeth and deliberately brought his ragged breathing under control. Would he have returned did he not carry a secret message for the Emir Yusef? Perhaps. Granada was the only home he had ever known. But he had long been absent, and

God knew he was much changed. Would he be welcomed by the Arab family that had raised him? Would they even recognise him after all these years?

Far below, the muezzin's thin voice rose in the call to evening prayer. The sun swelled into a bloody orange ball and dipped towards the hills in the west, spreading golden light over the rooftops, and Reynaud's chest grew tight. How he had loved this city as a boy, loved the exotic, spicy smells wafting from kitchens, the Jews' crowded bookstalls, the throb and hum of a busy Moorish kingdom. He had even grown to love the muezzin's chant.

He turned the grey stallion on to the sloping path, leaning back in his saddle as the descent steepened. By the time he reached the lightly guarded north gate, darkness shrouded him.

The lone guard waved him through the city walls. The moment he rode through the gate he reined the horse to a stop and sat motionless, listening to the sounds of the place where he had grown up. Lute music drifted from a nearby courtyard, punctuated by the sound of someone singing—a woman's voice, low and rich, the words half-Catalan, half-Arabic. He cocked his head, listening, and slowly inhaled the thick sweet scent of orange blossoms.

A pain keen as a lance pierced his heart. Despite his Templar vows, he still ached for the sound of a woman's voice, the comfort of a woman's soft body. He thought he had forgotten loneliness, but beneath his white surcoat he was still a man, was he not?

He shifted uneasily in the high-backed saddle. He

had lost something during the long years of fighting, something he could not name. After a time it had mattered not who was responsible for the pile of mangled corpses behind every city gate. Death smelled the same for Christian and Saracen.

A shadow danced against the whitewashed wall. He laid one hand on his sword hilt, studying the silent street of the shoemakers. Someone was following him.

No one could predict how the Arabs of Granada would greet a Christian Templar knight in their midst. A thief would want the gold weighting his saddlebags. Reynaud would kill the man, and that would be that. But if it was not the gold he was after…could someone know about the secret message he was carrying?

He stepped the nervous horse into the nearest alley, and when it split in two directions, he took the wider path, then doubled back, threading his way through narrow, twisting streets he only half-remembered.

Behind him, a gate latch clicked. Out of the corner of his eye he saw the scrolled-iron barrier swing open on noiseless hinges, then glimpsed a splash of crimson before an unseen hand slowly pushed the gate closed. The hair on the back of his neck prickled.

He studied the cobbled street. Even the scraping of the cicadas had ceased, and the feeling that someone watched him sent a snake crawling down his spine. He spurred the horse forwards, every nerve alert.

A shrouded figure glided from an alley and Reynaud automatically manoeuvred the stallion to block the man's path. Resting his hand on his sword, he bent forwards.

It was not a man, but a young woman!

He stared down at her. From under the hood of her black cloak she looked back at him with defiance in her eyes.

'What business brings you out this night?' he bit out.

'My own business,' she said calmly from behind her dark face veil. 'And none of yours.' She turned to move away, and he caught a whiff of perfume, a mix of sweet-scented roses and something darker. Musk, perhaps. He drew his sword and blocked her way.

'You should not be out alone. You should be safe in your house.' This was what he had fought for these long years, not only to free Jerusalem from the infidel, but to protect the civilised world. Protect women from the suffering he had seen, the horror of battle and the cruelty of depraved men.

'I do what I wish,' she said with a toss of her head. 'And it is not what you are thinking. You have no right to hold me here.'

He noted the cut and quality of her garments. Not a street woman, then. 'I would see you safely home.'

'You will not,' she replied. 'Who are you to order me about?'

'I am a knight of the Temple of Solomon.'

She peered up at him, focused on the red cross

stitched on his white Templar surcoat, then lifted her gaze to his.

'Have you travelled far?'

'From Antioch, in the Holy Land.'

She studied him with widening eyes. 'You must have seen wondrous places on your journey.'

Reynaud blinked at her words. 'Aye,' he said slowly, watching her eyes. 'Great cities and blood-soaked battlefields, where I learned to trust no one.'

'And now you come to Granada to waylay women?'

'Do not insult me!' he snapped.

'Then do not detain me! You have no right.' She pressed her balled-up fist against the flat of his sword and nudged it aside, then moved to step past him.

'Wait!'

She spun and pinned him with large grey eyes. 'Do you not mean wait, "if you please"?'

Reynaud swallowed hard. She was insolent. But he was being unchivalrous. 'I beg forgiveness. I have been too long on the battlefield.'

'Ah,' she breathed. 'Still, you are free to travel wherever you wish. I envy you.'

'Then you are but a foolish woman.'

Her frame stiffened. 'That,' she said, 'I am not.'

'Where is your father? Your husband?'

'I have no husband,' she replied quietly. 'And at this hour, my father is sleeping.'

'Does he know what his daughter is about?'

She sucked in a quick breath. 'Ah, no, he does not.'

A sour taste flooded his mouth and he spat to one side. 'He will whip you when he finds out.'

'That he will not. This is Granada. Women here have choices they do not enjoy elsewhere.'

His spine jolted upright. 'Choices? What choices? Women were created to beget children.'

Her eyes flashed. 'You are wrong. Women must—' Her hair escaped her head covering and tumbled past her shoulders in a satiny, midnight-dark mass. Still holding his gaze, she slowly drew aside her face veil.

Full, soft-looking lips curved slightly downwards at the corners. Her teeth shone white as pearls against her sun-bronzed skin. An iron crossbolt slammed into his heart. He could not draw breath.

He clenched his jaw. 'Get you gone.'

She raised her chin. 'No man orders me thus. Not even a Templar knight.'

She was small and delicate and her eyes were beautiful. He felt the gnawing of his body's hunger in every muscle and sinew.

As a Christian knight, pledged to celibacy, he avoided women. But as a man…God help him, as a man he looked upon her with desire licking at his body.

'Go,' he ordered.

She shot him a long venomous look, whirled and melted into the dark.

Gritting his teeth, Reynaud turned his mount towards the heart of the Moorish sector and the familiar house overlooking the city where he had grown up.

* * *

In the rambling palace Reynaud paused behind the latticed entrance to his foster uncle's quarters and tried to steady his heartbeat. Before he could speak, Hassam strode forwards, extending both his hands, and Reynaud was pulled into the older man's embrace.

'Welcome, Nephew! I feared never to see you again.' The older man released him and stepped back. 'You have changed much.'

Reynaud grasped the vizier's arm and held it tight. For a moment he could not speak. 'Uncle,' he managed. 'I have seen much that would age a man.'

Hassam smiled. 'Of that I have no doubt. A man is always anxious to leave his youth behind. Then, when he has outgrown his milk teeth and been blooded in battle, he longs for a return to innocence.' He smiled again, his teeth a flash of white in the lean, sharp-boned face. 'It is the same with all men.'

Reynaud studied his uncle. The spare frame outlined under the emerald silk tunic was still erect and proud, the movements agile, even graceful. Only the touch of silver in the dark hair betrayed Hassam's age. He must be nearly sixty winters. And even though it had been Hassam's preoccupied younger brother who had raised Reynaud as his foster son, Reynaud loved his uncle more than any man he had ever known.

'Come.' Hassam gestured to a low sofa covered with embroidered cushions. 'Sit with me. We have heard nothing of you for these twenty years. And besides,' he confided, 'I have my own reasons for speaking with you alone.'

Reynaud unbuckled his belt and carefully laid the sheathed sword on a carved wooden chest, then settled himself on the couch beside his uncle and waited while he signalled a young slave to bring coffee. 'What reasons?'

Hassam chuckled. 'You were ever direct, Nephew.'

'Your pardon, Uncle. I have not the time to be otherwise.'

'Nor have I.'

Reynaud accepted the tiny cup of fragrant dark liquid the servant proffered and waited until Hassam spoke quietly to the boy and gestured him away.

'I carry a message for Emir Yusef,' he said quietly.

The vizier nodded, cradling his coffee between thumb and forefinger, but he said nothing.

'For your ears only. As a Christian knight, I cannot deliver it in person.'

'Of course.'

Reynaud hesitated a split second. 'From the Templar master, Bertrand de Blanquefort, in Acre.'

Hassam's black eyebrows went up, but his face remained expressionless. The dark eyes that met Reynaud's were calculating.

'It is thought, Uncle, that you have Emir Yusef's ear. That you could deliver this message to him.'

'Perhaps. What would such a message concern? I would not play the traitor to Yusef.'

Reynaud held his uncle's gaze. 'The Templars

wish peace between Arab and Christian forces, Uncle. De Blanquefort would join forces with Granada to maintain a balance of power, and to establish a Templar presence in Spain.'

His uncle swallowed the last of his coffee and positioned the cup on the polished brass tray. 'Yes, I could convey your Grand Master's message to Emir Yusef.' He cast a speculative look at Reynaud and a broad smile lit his face.

'For a price.'

Reynaud ground his teeth. 'What price?'

Hassam cleared his throat. 'My daughter, Leonor, travels to Navarre to visit her great-aunt Alais of Moyanne. I will send an armed escort with her, but when she reaches the town, I fear for her. She will need protection.'

'Why?' Reynaud asked, his tone sharp.

'Think, man. She is an heiress, with lands in both Aragon and Navarre. She could be kidnapped. Forced to marry.'

Reynaud nodded. 'Raped, you mean. And married after. It is a common enough means for a landless knight to gain riches.'

'She is my only daughter,' Hassam said simply. 'I do not wish that for her.'

Again Reynaud nodded. 'You want me to protect her.'

'Aye.' Hassam grinned. 'That is the price.'

Reynaud groaned under his breath. The last thing he wanted was to be saddled with Hassam's daughter. He had not laid eyes on her for a score of years, but even as a child she had been a handful for her nurse-maids and tutors, even for her father. She was irre-pressible. And more clever than any young girl should be.

Besides, he had other, more important business in Moyanne. Business that would be hampered by keeping an eye on Hassam's daughter. He opened his mouth to protest, but his uncle suddenly rose.

'Ah, she is here. Leonor, we have a visitor.'

A slim young woman in an ankle-length scarlet tunic glided through the latticed entry, and Reynaud's heart stopped. Dumbstruck, he gazed at her as if in a dream.

It was the street woman!

Chapter Two

Reynaud rose from the sofa as courtesy demanded, his body on fire. They had met not an hour before, on the dark streets of Granada. Why could he not draw breath?

Did his uncle know that Leonor…?

No, it was not possible. Hassam would not allow it.

His uncle cleared his throat politely. 'Daughter, do you not remember your cousin Reynaud?'

As her father's words registered, her face changed. The feathery black lashes brushed her cheek, then lifted, and beneath the dark, arched brows her grey eyes widened. She stared at him, her mouth opening to speak, her lips trembling.

'Reynaud?' she whispered. 'Is it truly you? After all these years?' She reached to touch him, then faltered.

'It is,' he said, his voice clipped. His head spun.

It mattered not who she was; his physical response to her made him light-headed.

She stepped closer and peered up at him. Tears glittered in her eyes. 'What has happened to you?'

'After I left Granada I was made a squire in Vezelay, and taken on crusade to the Holy Land. Etienne de Tournay knighted me in the field.'

With a cry she took his face in her hands and stretched up to kiss his cheek. 'You sent no word, not one. Not a messenger, not even a letter in all these years. I thought you were dead!'

His throat closed. He wished he *were* dead. As custom dictated, he bent stiffly and brushed her forehead with his lips. Her skin tasted of roses.

What could he say?

With a wave of his hand Hassam motioned them both to be seated. Reynaud uneasily resumed his place on the sofa; after a covert glance at her father, Leonor perched on a square silk cushion at his feet.

A heavy, awkward silence descended. Leonor refused to meet his eyes, and in the oppressive quiet the uneven beating of his own heart pounded in his ear like a Saracen war drum.

After an interminable minute, she raised her head. 'Now that you have returned—'

'I have not returned,' he said shortly. 'I travel the world on missions for the Templar Grand Master. This is but one chapter in an ever-changing book. I belong nowhere.'

'You are welcome always in Granada,' Hassam interjected.

A rush of warmth swept through him. Under his surcoat his heart swelled with a bittersweet pain. He must leave this place, and soon. He would not dishonour Hassam's daughter by revealing what he knew of her, yet he could not lie to his uncle.

Leonor wrapped her arms around her folded legs, resting her chin on her knees. 'Perhaps you would tell me now of your adventures?' Still, she would not look at him.

He frowned at the edge in her voice. 'I will not. The things I have seen are not fit for a woman's ears.'

'My ears are not so delicate,' she murmured. She lifted her head and pinned him with her gaze. 'Not all women are weak.'

'And in truth,' he muttered, 'you are not like all women.'

Her grey eyes sparked with anger. 'So, you are now a Templar knight. It was always your dream to become a knight, was it not? That is why you left Granada. Was it not?'

He ignored the bite in her question.

'Have you other dreams beyond fighting battles? It must take great courage to impose your will on others,' she said. The venom in her tone made him flinch. Hassam stared at his daughter with puzzled eyes.

'Courage I still have,' he said quietly. 'But as for dreams, I...I no longer believe in dreams. I believe in nothing save my horse and the bite of my sword.'

She sat motionless, her grey eyes clouding. 'Then

you are adrift, like a boat with no sail, tossed on the sea.'

Reynaud groaned inwardly. He was more than adrift. He had lost more than hope in his journeys. He had lost the sense of belonging. Of knowing who, or what, he was.

And now, of knowing who *she* was. Was Leonor his uncle Hassam's treasured daughter? Or a woman of the streets?

Her lips curved in an odd little half-smile. 'I long to see the world and its wonders. To do this, I must leave my father's house.'

Reynaud held her eyes. Did she comprehend none of what he had said earlier? Did she not care about her proper place as a woman? True, his own restless life made him feel as if he were drifting, a twig carried on a river that flowed he knew not where. She, at least, had a home.

'The world is not a pretty place.'

She smiled again, and his heartbeat stuttered. How he wondered at her physical effect on him!

'I understand that all too well,' she said, her tone cool. 'I am often at Emir Yusef's court.' She held his gaze, daring him to betray her to Hassam. 'I speak three languages, and I am invited to the palace to play chess and join the musicians. Life is to be enjoyed. Do you not think so?'

'You live in a household of wealth and learning,' he said tightly. 'You have no idea of life outside of Granada.'

Her eyes flashed fire. 'Do not lecture me as if I

were a child.' She glanced at her father, then looked down, crushing the silk of her tunic in her fist. 'I do want to see the outside world. To learn. Is that wrong?'

'No. Not wrong. But foolish.' He studied her flowing red tunic, the sheer face veil she had again drawn to one side. 'Outside of Granada, you would stand out, like a blossoming orange tree in the desert.'

'That I know. It is because I am…different.'

She was certainly that. Like an exquisite jewel among rubble, enticing and unattainable.

'You are only half-Arab,' he reminded. 'And you have grown up in the privileged household of Hassam. Benjamin the Scholar tutored you in history and philosophy, and I recall that your Christian mother taught you writing and languages before you could walk properly.'

'And music,' she added, her eyes glowing.

He tore his gaze away from her. 'You are old enough to be married,' he said bluntly. 'How is it you are not?'

Her soft smile sent a wave of prickly sensation straight to his groin.

'Were it not for the Emir's protection…' she shot a look at her father '…I would have been married off long ago, a plum in some prince's garden of wives. As it is, I am fortunate to have attained seven and twenty winters yet untouched by a man.'

'Hassam must have an understanding heart,' he said drily.

She gave her nodding father a wry smile. 'I think my father's heart is not the reason. Benjamin says it is because my mind is one hundred years old and sharp as a wolf's teeth. Suitors leave my father's receiving room tongue-tied and shaking their heads.'

'You know little of men,' he said. 'They are not so easily deterred.'

She raised her chin in a gesture he remembered from long ago. 'Doubt me not, Reynaud. I know a great deal about men. I have studied my father and the men who visit him. And guests and dignitaries, both Christian and Arab, who flock to the vizier's palace. I watch and I listen, and I evaluate.'

'Why?' The question grated past stiff lips.

Hassam rose and moved to the latticed entrance and signalled for more coffee. Leonor shot a glance at his back.

'Because,' she said in an undertone, 'if I cannot have a man to whom I can give my whole heart and soul, then I want no man at all.'

Reynaud rolled his eyes towards the ceiling and shifted uncomfortably on the pillow-strewn couch. Was she in truth untouched? That was hard to believe, considering where he had encountered her earlier this evening.

His attraction to her disturbed him more than he could admit. He gritted his teeth against the insistent swelling of his manhood.

'And Hassam agrees to this…this dream of yours? Freedom to choose one's own husband is rarer than swords of Byzantine silver.'

She studied the retreating figure of her father and lowered her voice. 'He does not yet know of it. But I also make other choices,' she said, pronouncing the last word with special care. 'Not one word of this to my father,' she whispered hurriedly. 'The man has worries enough with the fate of Granada balanced on his plate.'

Reynaud jerked his head up and caught her pleading gaze. 'Not one word about what? Tell me the truth, Leonor.'

'I…' She leaned closer. 'I visit the gypsies at night. That is why I was on the street earlier.'

Unconsciously he clenched his fists against his thighs. 'What? Why?'

'I wish to learn their songs. Gypsy songs.'

'Why?' he snapped again.

'Because I love their strange, sad music. And I plan—' She broke off.

Suspicion lowered his voice to a growl. 'What do you plan?'

She studied the satin slippers peeking from under her tunic.

'Tomorrow I begin a journey, as I'm sure Father told you. He will fuss and pace about his quarters until he receives word that I am safe in Moyanne with Great-Aunt Alais, but he agrees to let me go. Not for all the jewels in Persia would I add to his worries.'

'And what,' Reynaud said carefully, 'might those worries be?'

Leonor ignored the question and tipped her head

to one side, resting her cheek against her bent knees. 'Father need not know of the adventure I dream of,' she murmured. 'That is for myself alone.'

Adventure? Reynaud's spine tingled. She had not changed a jot since she was a child. She was far too clever for her own good. She was headstrong. And more stubborn than the worst of Hassam's pack mules.

'Tomorrow,' she continued, her voice distant, 'when the sun spreads apricot light—oh! Isn't that a lovely word, "apricot"? When the sun spreads apricot light across the sky, I will spread my wings outside the walls of Granada.'

No wonder Hassam wanted protection for her. Her head was full of dreams. She must never seek the outside world. It was ugly, dirty, full of depravity. Leonor was yet untouched by the degradation he had seen, by the sins and selfish manoeuvring of men. He would save her from that world.

If he could.

The problem was she did not want *to be saved.*

He sighed in defeat. She was an exquisitely beautiful woman, her skin smooth as fine ivory, her every movement graceful. Sensual.

He did not like her talk of adventure. *What was she planning to do, apart from visiting her great-aunt?* He would have to watch her every moment. Clenching his teeth, he turned away just as Hassam returned to the room. Like it or not, he had pledged his word to his uncle.

Therefore, so be it.

Chapter Three

Reynaud removed his sword belt and mail shirt and leggings, stretched out on the soft sleeping couch and willed himself to tame his roiling thoughts. In the years he had been away, Leonor had grown from a playful sprite of a girl into a heart-stoppingly beautiful woman. He could not forget the scent of her hair, the sheen of her skin.

And he could not forget how foolishly eager she was to leave the safety of Granada. Her innocence was dangerous. She knew nothing of the harsh world outside this luxurious palace in this enlightened kingdom. In truth, he himself felt out of place surrounded by the opulence of his Uncle Hassam's home.

In truth, he no longer knew where he belonged. He laid his head wherever his Templar orders took him, even to Hassam's spacious home with its brightly tiled courtyards and the sound of splashing fountains in every room. He was to deliver the Templar proposal to Emir Yusef, then await orders for his next destination after Moyanne, to be delivered by someone in Yusef's employ. But he did not yet know who. Neither did he know the final destination of the Templar gold he carried.

He tried to soothe his restless spirit with the trickle of fountains and the carefree chirping of night birds nesting among the branches of tamarisk trees, but memories of battle followed him wherever he went. The bloodshed, the unending senseless slaughter, the stench of burning fortresses and rotting corpses—it sickened him. With all his heart he wished he could be washed clean of his sins.

Abruptly he sat bolt upright. Was he still a pious follower of Almighty God? Or was he now a mercenary killer available to the highest bidder? At some point he needed to know what, and who, he really was. Otherwise, he could forge no other future for himself.

The next morning Reynaud gazed across the flat brown plain into the hazy distance, then reined in his grey destrier and waited for the armed escort Hassam had sent to guard Leonor. The way was clear; he had already scouted ahead for bandits.

For a long while all he could see were puffs of dust rolling towards him. No sound broke the quiet but the wind whispering through the pine scrub and the thud of hoofbeats against the hard-baked ground. Some minutes later, two horses and a mule plodded into view, laden with travel chests and surrounded by the Arab warriors. He raised one hand in silent greeting.

A large dun horse carried a tall elderly man, his black robe flapping behind his bent frame like the wings of an ancient crow. Reynaud had to smile. Benjamin of Toledo, his old tutor!

The other rider, well mounted on a cream-coloured Arab mare, wore leather riding boots, a short, drab tunic and a white turban and head veil. He studied the slight figure through narrowed eyes and his heart lurched. It was Leonor!

Every nerve jolted to attention. Travelling in disguise made good sense, but by the look of Leonor's jaunty smile she was truly revelling in her masquerade.

She had always loved masquerades.

He signalled to Sekir, Hassam's personal body-guard, and pressed among the Arab warriors until he came face to face with his cousin. She flicked a glance at him, studied his chainmail hauberk, then his helmet. After a long moment her shining eyes met his and his heart stuttered.

'You are following us,' she observed, her voice accusing.

'True, and not true. I travel with you, but at a distance, to watch for bandits. I promised Hassam I would look to your welfare.'

She frowned. 'I do not want you to look to my welfare. You, with your battle-scarred soul and your distrust of the world, would never let me do *anything*.

Particularly not what I have in mind.' With an eloquent lift of her dark eyebrows, she flapped her reins and rode on past him.

Stung, Reynaud circled his horse to block her path.

Thoughtfully she pursed her lips. The gesture sent red-hot needles dancing along the skin behind his neck.

He remembered that look. Even as a boy that gaze could make his heart thud in his bony chest like a smithy's hammer. With Leonor he'd never known what to expect. How she had loved playing tricks.

Benjamin rode up, peering at her from under his bushy grey eyebrows. 'Ay, Jehovah,' he grumbled. 'Why do you stop in the middle of the road?' The old man paid no attention to Reynaud; apparently he did not recognise his old student.

'I was…reviewing my plan,' Leonor replied, a happy lilt in her voice.

Reynaud's belly knotted. What plan? What was she up to besides visiting her great-aunt?

The old man's black eyes rounded. 'What, again? Can you not ride and plan at the same time?'

She laughed softly. 'I can do many things at the same time, Benjamin. As you well know.'

'Do not remind me,' Benjamin growled. He tried in vain to hide the fond look in his dark eyes.

Reynaud groaned inwardly. When she was young, Leonor had tied her father into knots. Now she was grown, and so comely that the soft curves of her body made his skin burn. Keeping an eye on her would be a challenge.

Considering his body's response to her, it would be an ordeal by fire! He nodded to Benjamin, kicked the grey warhorse into a trot and turned his face towards the rocky grey hills to the west. What devil had prompted him to agree to protecting her?

He circled around behind the party of riders to make sure they were not followed through the remote mountain pass leading to the walled town of Moyanne.

He knew the town. As a youth, in Moyanne he had learned about wine from Burgundy and women from…everywhere.

The old hunger bit into his loins and he straightened in the saddle and willed his thoughts elsewhere. He had fought too hard to become a Templar knight to sacrifice his honour for a mere itch of the flesh.

With undisguised relish Leonor studied the moss-covered stone walls enclosing the small village of Moyanne, then peered upward at the dark stone castle on the hilltop beyond. After the bustling streets and brilliant-coloured tiled buildings of Granada, this pretty little town looked as if nothing had changed for a hundred years. Surely Great-Aunt Alais must lead a peaceful life in such a place.

The flock of sparrows in her belly fluttered to life, and she nudged the cream-coloured mare forwards. Some minutes later the two horses and the mule clopped over the castle's planked drawbridge and through the raised portcullis to enter a cobblestone bailey surrounded by a hodgepodge of wooden buildings. From the closest drifted the sound of clanging metal, followed by the hiss of steam. The smithy's quarters.

She studied the inhabitants of the bailey. Stable boys, washing women, even a sour-faced priest. Unconsciously she looked for an even more sour-faced Reynaud, but there was no sign of her moody cousin.

Good. She was not a child who needed tending.

Pages ran forwards to help them dismount and unload the baggage from the pack mule tied behind Benjamin's mount. The instant she slid off the cream mare an icy shard of fear stabbed beneath her breastbone.

She was here at last. She could turn her dream into a triumph…or she could make such a fool of herself that no one, not even Benjamin, would ever speak to her again. Worse, perhaps they would laugh at her.

Her chest felt as if jagged rocks were piling up behind her ribs. She was not just frightened, she was petrified!

She swallowed hard. 'Benjamin, I am…I am somewhat afraid.'

The old man sent her a quick sideways look. 'All things have their price, little one. Especially great adventures.' His black eyes twinkled.

She frowned at him. 'Oh, Ben… In truth, I am *very* afraid.'

Benjamin um-hummed beside her. 'Tell me,' he urged in his soft rumbly voice.

'I cannot explain, exactly. All my life I have

dreamed of the time when I would leave my father's house and seek my own destiny.'

'Ah, and here you are, are you not?'

She turned her gaze away from his narrow wrinkled face and focused instead on the portcullis behind them. Any moment Reynaud would clatter over the drawbridge. She did not want him to know she was afraid. She resented his dutiful overprotectiveness. And his disapproval of her.

'One part of me can hardly wait!' she blurted. 'Another part of me wants to turn back and ride to the safety of my father's house.'

'Which do you want most?' her tutor queried in his gravelly voice.

She drew in a shaky gulp of air. 'I have ridden all the way from Granada to follow the joyous art. *Gai saber* it is called in the courts of Aquitaine. What I want most is…is to try.'

Benjamin merely nodded and his black eyes softened. 'And, so?' he murmured.

Yes, she would try. She would do it this very night, exactly as she'd planned these many months. She caught a passing page by the sleeve and tugged him to attention. 'I would speak with the Lady Alais. In private.'

The boy's eyes widened for an instant, then he raced off and disappeared through a narrow doorway. Leonor lifted her harp, wrapped in a nest of carpets carried on the pack mule, squared her shoulders and marched towards the castle entrance.

Chapter Four

From the rampart overlooking the bailey Reynaud watched for a moment longer, his pulse jumping in an irregular beat at the sight of the slim girlish figure in the white turban.

With a curse he turned away from the battlement and descended the narrow circular staircase. He had important business here in Moyanne besides looking after Leonor. Whoever was to contact him while he was here, with instructions for disposing of the Templar gold hidden in his saddlebags, would use the coded password de Blanquefort had given him. Beyond that, his Grand Master had told him nothing.

So he must wait. But each time he laid eyes on Leonor, a warm rush of blood beat in his chest, and the darkness inside him lifted. Though his spirit was weary, his body was becoming frighteningly alive.

In the great hall the huge stone fireplace stood empty. Moyanne's summer heat left the evening air balmy and still until long past Lauds. It reminded him of Syria, except that nights there were never quiet.

The smoky flames of rushlights illuminated the noisy company assembled in Count Henri's hall. The count and his lady-wife Alais welcomed him with unfeigned cordiality, yet again he felt out of place, neither Frankish nor Arab.

To his surprise, Reynaud found himself sitting in the place of honour at Count Henri's right hand. Henri himself, the count confided, had served as a Hospitaller. He had a fondness for knights of a military order, even the rival order of Knights Templar.

A portly wine server made his leisurely rounds from the raised dais to the linen-covered trestle tables abutting each end. Reynaud drank deeply from his overflowing cup and tried to screen out the noise and bustle. Lords and ladies in silks and ribbons, knights, churchmen in sombre robes, even children were crowded together in the warm, sweat-scented room.

He focused on the nimble juggler in the centre area. Dressed in tight red hose and a belled cap, the fellow tossed yellow apples into the air, bouncing them off his arms before catching them.

Count Henri leaned towards him. 'Later,' he said in an undertone, 'there will be dancing.'

Reynaud hid a grimace. Before he had made his vows, dancing with a woman had brought him pleasure. Now he contented himself with watching the assembled guests for a glimpse of Leonor. When he had assured himself that she was safe and protected, he would count the hours before Compline and then sleep.

He gulped the rich, sweet liquid in his wine cup and tried to concentrate on his host's conversation over the rattle of eating knives and bursts of laughter. But his gaze moved from face to face, for the thousandth time studying knight and noble lady alike.

Where was Leonor?

'Drink up, Reynaud,' the count urged. 'Our meal will be…' he slanted an amused look at Lady Alais '…delayed somewhat. My lady-wife's favourite hound whelped this afternoon. She promised a pup to the cook.'

Lady Alais covered her husband's hand with her own. 'Cook could not decide which of the six she preferred, my dear. Truth to tell, neither could I. They are all quite handsome.'

She glanced at Reynaud. 'Perhaps you, Sir Reynaud, would like a companion?'

Reynaud shook his head at the tall, still elegant older woman in the simply cut, dark blue gown. 'Not I, lady. I travel overmuch to care for a pup. Neither have I time in which to train it.'

In truth, he found it difficult to stay in one place for very long. He was footloose, and when he had time on his hands he tended to brood. He welcomed orders that sent him on another journey.

Alais gave him a gentle smile. 'A pity. I fear there are too many pups to keep, but I cannot bear to see them drowned.' She turned to the heavy-set man on her left. 'My Lord Robert, have you a hound?'

Henri chuckled and saluted his wife with his raised wine cup. He drank, then winked at Reynaud. 'I'll not drown them,' he said in an undertone. 'But if she thinks I will, it will spur her to find homes for the little brutes all the quicker. Women, bless them, are soft-hearted creatures when it comes to young things.'

The count's face stilled for an instant. 'Perhaps it would not be thus if she had had babes of her own.'

'You have no offspring, my lord?'

'I have a son,' Henri said quietly. 'His mother died in birthing him. He was a man full grown when Alais came to me as a bride.'

'Does he still live?'

'Perhaps. If God wills it. I have not seen him for thirty summers. He was fostered with my brother, Roger of St Bertrand, at Carcassonne and thence travelled across the sea to Jerusalem. A handsome lad he was, before he left.'

'I met many from Navarre while in the Holy Land. How was your son called?'

'Bernard,' the count replied. 'But he was not a knight of your order. He was also a Hospitaller.'

Before he could question the count further, a young boy appeared at the far end of the hall, a harp slung over one slim shoulder. A floppy velvet cap drooped over his features.

Count Henri's eyes went wide with surprise, but Reynaud's heart lifted. A troubadour! He had not

heard a troubadour ballad since he rode out of
Vezelay as a squire twenty years past.

And God knew his weary heart was hungry for
solace.

Leonor paused at the entrance to the main hall and
waited for her aunt's signal from the head table.
Quickly she adjusted her grip on the harp and pushed
a stubborn strand of hair up under her green velvet
cap. Benjamin gently squeezed her arm. 'Go with
God, little one,' he whispered. *'Shalom.'*

The moment had come. Her heart leaped like an
untamed hawk straining at its jesses.

The sting of poetry had always sent a thrill to her
midsection, like being blown aloft by a holy breath.
When she sang the words of her heart, the world
stopped turning, and for a brief moment she felt at
one with all humankind.

But only in the land of Aquitaine, where Great
Eleanor ruled, was there a woman troubadour. It was
whispered that at Eleanor's court there were even
women poets!

Yet this was Moyanne, not Aquitaine. Perhaps
they would not welcome a woman troubadour. Her
mouth went dry as a thistle.

At her aunt's beckoning gesture, she started forwards, her heart thudding in her ears. If she glanced
down at the loose-fitting silk tunic, it would be
visibly fluttering over her chest with each beat.
Better not to look.

She raised her chin and gazed across the hall.

Next to her Uncle Henri sat Reynaud, tall and dark-haired in his white surcoat. She focused on the eight-pointed crimson cross emblazoned on his chest and willed her shaking limbs to carry her forwards, towards him.

Reynaud's body suddenly went cold. That was no young minstrel. That was Leonor gliding towards him! And, God save her, she was wearing trousers! What was she thinking, entering the hall in a man's garb? And carrying a harp?

Women did not perform in public. Certainly not a high-born woman like Leonor, educated in languages and versed in court etiquette. Surely she knew better. Henri's guests would not listen to the music a woman would make. They would shout until she ceased singing.

Unable to breathe, Reynaud followed her progress through the horde of servants and guests in the crowded hall. She looked so small. And defenceless. Her simple embroidered tunic reached almost to the floor, and on her head she wore a matching green cap with a jaunty feather. But under the boy's apparel she was unmistakably female! The delicate bones in her face, her graceful, sinuous motions screamed Woman.

His breath choked off. Did no one see what was so apparent to him? She was safe only if none realised she was female! He ground his teeth in an agony of frustration. It was too late to stop her.

The room buzzed in anticipation. Leonor advanced to the centre and bowed courteously to the count and Lady Alais.

Alais leaned towards her husband. 'My dear, this is the harper I told you of earlier.' At her significant look, Henri turned his full attention towards the youth.

Leonor sank on to a round wooden stool and bent her head to check her tuning. The hall quieted.

Under his surcoat Reynaud began to sweat. The crowd would not receive her well. How could he protect her in this foolhardy venture? He had stashed his sword belt, along with those of the other knights, with the burly guard at the hall entrance. Now, he had no weapon.

Silence dropped over the hall like soft mist. When the hush thickened, Leonor straightened, pulled the harp back on to her right shoulder and plucked a single chord.

Then she began to sing.

In spite of his pounding heart, he could not shut out her voice. What beautiful music! Her voice was low and melodious, rich in timbre. A woman's voice, not the voice of the girl he remembered.

And such poetry! The words, in Arabic, described the soaring of a lark, the flight of a heart in ecstasy. The verses were so beautifully wrought that his chest tightened.

The backs of his eyelids began to burn. Not since his youth had a song touched him so deeply. His throat ached. He wanted to weep. The throb of her harp through his soul was almost painful, the longing aroused in him gnawing at his vitals.

Ah, he could stand no more. He clenched his

hands until his knuckles cracked, and then, mercifully, the mesmerising voice and the murmur of the harp faded into silence.

He waited, scarcely able to draw breath.

Leonor dipped her head in a subtle obeisance to the count and Lady Alais but remained motionless on her stool. Reynaud could not take his eyes off her.

No one made a sound. At his elbow, Count Henri gaped open-mouthed at the slim figure in the centre of the hall. 'By the saints,' he breathed into the lingering hush.

She raised her head at last, and Reynaud saw that her grey eyes glittered with unshed tears.

Pandemonium broke out. Nobles and commoners alike banged their wine cups on the table and cheered until they were hoarse.

Reynaud drew in an unsteady breath. She had enchanted them. Thank God. *Thank God!*

She rose, stepped to the high table, and knelt on one knee before Count Henri and Lady Alais. Then she reached a small, fine-boned hand up to her feathered cap and with a quick motion drew it off and placed it across her heart.

Hair the colour of black silk tumbled down her slender back.

The crowd gasped. 'A woman!' someone shouted. 'The minstrel is a woman!'

Reynaud was on his feet before he knew what he was doing, intending to head towards the wooden rack of swords at the front of the hall. Never before had he felt such an overpowering need to protect someone.

He halted as an underlying truth burned into his brain. Never before had he felt such a gut-deep yearning to touch another human spirit.

But a woman? His vows forbade it. He had to escape whatever it was pulling his soul to hers.

The shouting of the dinner guests echoed in the stone hall and then, abruptly, all noise ceased. His body began to tremble.

She would play again.

He didn't think he could stand it.

Chapter Five

Reynaud rose to escape from the table, but the count turned to him. 'Stay, man,' he commanded in an undertone. With a hand heavy as a mace, he pressed Reynaud back into his seat at the linen-covered table.

The clatter of eating knives and drinking cups ceased. Quiet descended over the crowded hall and Reynaud clamped his teeth together. Without discourtesy to his host, he could not escape.

Leonor adjusted the tuning on one peg, idly strummed her slim fingers once, twice across the strings in a seemingly spontaneous melodic pattern. A tune gradually emerged, and then a counter-melody bloomed underneath it.

Her long fingers floated over the harp strings, her slender hands like winged birds in motion. Her hair, dark as midnight, fell forwards to obscure her features, and when she brushed it back in the quick, unconscious gesture he remembered, something tore at his gut.

She was seven and twenty now, and she took his breath away!

The last notes of the song resonated off the thick stone walls, and Leonor lifted her head and met his gaze. Beneath the dark, arched brows her smoke-grey eyes sent him a challenging look.

His throat closed.

'So, my friend.' Count Henri chuckled. 'I wager you did not recognise her at first. She is a feast for the eyes, is she not?'

Reynaud sat without moving, unable to speak.

'My lord?' Leonor's low, clear voice at his side jerked him to attention.

'Since you have lately returned from the land across the sea, is there some music you would hear? The count asks it in your honour.'

Reynaud flicked a glance at Count Henri, who was grinning at him over his wine cup. Damn the man. The count bobbed his head as if to say, *Well? Does she not make an exquisite troubadour?*

Reynaud swallowed over a lump the size of the juggler's apple. 'I do have a request.' He watched Henri settle his bent form back in his chair, his lips twitching in anticipation.

Leonor's grey eyes lifted to his. 'And that is?'

He leaned towards her and lowered his voice. 'I wish to talk with you. In private.'

Count Henri choked out, 'Talk?' He eyed Reynaud in exasperation.

Reynaud nodded. 'Talk,' he repeated. He shot the count a swift look. 'I mean no discourtesy, my lord,' he murmured. 'For the moment, might I have your indulgence?'

A frown creased Count Henri's ruddy forehead. 'Indulgence?' In the next instant his eyes brightened. 'Oh! Yes, I see now. You young cousins would be private, of course! Forgive my slowness.' He tapped his skull with one beringed finger. 'My age, you know. Go now, and talk.'

Leonor's eyes widened. 'But, Uncle—'

'Whsst, child. Do as I say. You will be glad for it, I promise you.' Henri waved her away. 'Go! *Go*! *Shoo*!'

Leonor reached across the table and patted the old man's hand. 'Never before have I been allowed to be private with a man, Uncle. Thank you!'

At Henri's startled look, Leonor sent him a dazzling smile. 'I am sure the experience will greatly further my education.'

Reynaud suppressed the laugh that rose in his throat. A man stood little chance against that one.

Leonor beckoned. 'Will you follow me, my lord?'

In the narrow passageway just off the great hall, Leonor turned to face him. 'We are private now, my lord. What did you wish?'

His face betrayed no emotion save for an odd tightness about his mouth, but his eyes spoke volumes. They were green as the winter sea, and wary. He reminded her of a falcon her father had once trained—disciplined and powerful. He looked

like one who could kill a man in a heartbeat, then fall
to his knees and pray for forgiveness.

He stood looking at her while she studied his
strained, unsmiling face in silence. Never in her entire
life had she wondered so about a man. His features
were young, but his eyes looked old. Something
about Reynaud drew her like a silver coin to a lode-
stone.

'Why do you look so sour?' she murmured.

'I have my reasons,' he said shortly.

'I would wager you have dark places inside you
that few, if any, have plumbed. Rey, I do not wish to
be your enemy.'

He took a step forwards. For all the strength of his
broad shoulders and length of limb, he was oddly
graceful. Would he dance as beautifully as he
moved?

A slow, delicious heat crept into her belly. She
wanted to touch him. *What was she thinking?*

She forced herself to look into his face. 'You
wished to speak to me?'

Reynaud fought the impulse to reach out and drag
her against his chest. His hands ached to twine his
fingers through that silky hair. 'Leonor, you need not
address me as "my lord".'

'"My lord" implies no allegiance, only the respect
due to a knight of a holy order.'

'Knight I am. Lord, I am not. I am landless, as you
well know. Adrift, as you said before.'

'Landless, perhaps,' she said, her voice soft as
leaves, 'but not bereft of prospects, I would think.

There is some reason for your presence in Moyanne, is there not? Other than my father's concern for me, that is.'

Her candour startled him. She looked steadily into his eyes with no hint of artifice. Reynaud had forgotten how direct Leonor could be, even as a child. Then, too, she could hide her thoughts as well as he could.

'You know I am bastard-born. Brought to Hassam's house at birth in a basket of woven reeds. Prospects for such as myself are rare as roses in hell.'

She continued to regard him with eyes soft as grey velvet.

'Still…' She paused and unconsciously rimmed her lips with the tip of her tongue. 'If it does not displease you, I will yet call you "my lord".'

Reynaud's heart stuttered. Displease him! If she only knew. Desire heated his loins. A whiff of her fragrance, jasmine-sweet and faintly musky, reached his nostrils and he shut his eyes to savour the scent. He felt himself grow hard with wanting her.

He twisted away and stared at the stone floor beneath his feet, commanding his body to obey him. He must break the spell she cast, must move away from her. He took a step backward.

'Stay, Reynaud. I have offended you?'

'I—no. You offend no one.' *It is I who offends.* For a moment he forgot he was a Templar. A warrior-monk, pledged to celibacy.

No, there was more to it than that. Leonor was young and happy. A joyous being, eager for life. He was shackled not only by his vows, but by bitterness and distrust. Being near her cast a shadow on her gaiety, her joy in thinking all was well with the world. He would always drag her down.

Leonor closed the short distance between them and laid her hand on his arm. 'You wished to talk?' she reminded a third time.

Ah, yes, talk. 'Leonor, what are you about, posing as a minstrel in your uncle's house?' He spoke roughly.

'Posing! I am not "posing", I am performing as a troubadour. There is naught wrong in it. It has been my dream all my life, to travel and play music and see some of the world.'

'It is dangerous.'

'Why? Because I am a woman?'

'Aye.'

'Why should a woman exist only to be locked away in a prison of some man's making? A woman is *not* created only to pleasure a man. A woman is created to be herself.'

Reynaud clenched his fists at his sides. 'That is laughable.'

'That is *not* laughable! I love music, as you well remember. I wish to share it.'

'You can share it in Granada. In the privacy of your father's house.'

She propped her small hands on her hips. 'I wish to travel beyond Granada. I am curious about the world.'

He scowled down at her. 'You were always curious. I expected you would grow out of it.'

'Well, I did not,' she snapped. 'I am interested in things besides pleasing a man.'

By the saints and angels, did she not understand? 'You are reaching for disaster. Being a troubadour is not for a woman. Especially not one such as you.'

'You are wrong, Rey. Your view is jaded because of your own inner wounds. I will not let your distrust of the world spoil my dream. Besides there is naught you can do.'

'Your father—'

'Will not know.'

'I fear for you. You do…the unexpected. You know nothing of the world.'

'I am learning,' she snapped. 'You should be pleased for me.'

He gritted his teeth. 'I am not pleased.'

'Is that what you wished to say to me?'

'Aye,' he said in a hard voice.

She straightened her spine. 'Well, then, *my lord,* is there a song you would hear?'

Reynaud groaned. 'We had no minstrels in the Holy Land. God knows, we had little cause for singing.'

She nodded in understanding and sent him a half-smile. 'Since you had no minstrels, your heart must be hungry.'

He flinched as if struck. His jaw muscles tightened. No one had ever come nearer the truth.

'I will sing for you three tunes in the Catalan style, and you may judge which you like best.' She tugged him to face her and gazed up at him, her usually downturned mouth curving so deliciously he wanted to put his hand over her lips to hide them from his sight.

'Do not be angry with me, Rey. I seek only to be happy in this life, as do you.' She moved towards the doorway.

Reynaud moved to block her way. 'How would one such as you know what I seek in this life? Do you think making oneself happy is all there is?'

Leonor brushed away both questions with a wave of her hand. 'Come,' she urged again. 'Your songs await within.'

At her entrance, a cheer went up. Leonor inclined her head in acknowledgement, then took up her harp. Reynaud stood off to one side in the shadows, his mind in turmoil.

He tried to concentrate on the sound of the harp, the words of the verse half-sung, half-spoken in the blend of Sephardic and Arabic tongues known as Ladino. Something about a knight and four maidens. He glanced around him at the avid dinner guests in the over-warm hall. The men were entranced.

She began another song, a lai in triple time, the rhythm an intricate variation of the Arab *zajal*. Reynaud struggled to close his ears to the entrancing sound.

He leaned against the hard stone wall at his back, shut his eyes and steeled his spirit to listen to the seductive rise and fall of Leonor's voice. Her final song cut deep. The heartrending melody full of longing and passion wound its way into his gut. His throat closed suddenly into an aching knot.

And then a line of verse leaped into his consciousness. *'Know you the silver swan?'*

Instantly, his entire body stiffened, his heart plunging into an irregular thumping. He stared across the room at Leonor. By all that was holy, she had sung the coded words de Blanquefort had entrusted to him.

Thunderstruck, he could not make a sound.

Chapter Six

Benjamin looked up from his writing table as the sound of Leonor's harp, and then cheers, drifted to him from the hall below. He cocked his head, listening with undisguised pleasure.

Good. She had been accepted. Nay, revered, by the sound of shouts and the din of banging cups. Excellent! If she wished, his precious lamb could make her way from castle to court with her art. Now the whole world lay at Leonor's fingertips.

A shadow fell across the open doorway. Benjamin started, and a blot of ink fell on the page before him. 'Who comes?' His voice grated in the silence.

The Templar stepped across the threshold. The knight's wintry green eyes flicked to meet Benjamin's gaze. *'Shalom.'*

Benjamin blinked. 'And to you, peace also.'

Reynaud studied his old tutor, his lips widening into a broad smile. 'Greetings, Benjamin. *Alea jacta est.*'

Benjamin's black eyes snapped. 'What's that you say?'

'That was the first Latin sentence you ever taught me. Do you not remember?'

Benjamin half-rose from his seat. His gaze travelled from Reynaud's face to the scarlet cross stitched on the front of his surcoat, then dropped to his sword belt.

'So I see,' Benjamin murmured. 'Truly, the die *is* cast.'

He stood and clasped Reynaud in an embrace so tight the old man wheezed for breath.

'Gently, my son, gently. Your mail shirt cuts the skin. It is like grasping a tree to one's breast!'

Reynaud laughed. 'A tree, am I?'

Benjamin beamed up at him. 'Very like. Thou art a man, *in esse*. Now I wish to hear what you are doing here in Moyanne? I know about Hassam asking protection for Leonor…now I would know the rest of it. The truth.'

'I was sent. By the Templar master, Bertrand de Blanquefort, in Acre.'

'Acre,' Benjamin breathed. He raked crabbed fingers through his thick grey beard. 'And how goes it in Acre?'

'Well enough,' Reynaud answered. 'Christian fights Christian for power in Jerusalem. How goes it in Granada?'

The old man smiled. 'Well enough. Brother fights brother, as you well remember. Arab fights Christian and Arab as well. Al-Andalus cannot long survive with such division.'

'Nor can Jerusalem.' Reynaud eyed the older man. 'The pomegranate will be devoured, seed by seed. Think you that men are greedy for power, or just fools?'

'Fools. Greedy for power, yes, but fools. And that is dangerous.'

'I fear you are right,' Reynaud said on a sigh. 'Hassam taught me to think first and draw my blade second. But in Outremer, one does not long hold to that philosophy and live. Now I strike first and ask afterwards.'

Benjamin said nothing. Gesturing for Reynaud to sit, he blotted up the spilled ink and quickly poured two cups of wine from the wooden pitcher at his elbow. He handed one across the writing table to Reynaud. 'To your health.'

Reynaud lifted his cup. 'And yours.'

The two men studied each other. At last Benjamin cleared his throat.

Reynaud rose, set his wine cup on the table and bent close to the older man. 'Know you the silver swan?' he enunciated carefully.

'Eh? What? What are you talking about, a swan? What has a swan to do with anything?'

Satisfied, Reynaud patted the man's bony shoulder. Benjamin knew nothing about de Blanquefort's coded phrase. For the first time in his life he felt he was the teacher and Benjamin the student.

Deliberately he changed the subject. 'Tell me of Leonor.'

Just speaking her name brought an unexpected rush of warmth to his chest.

'Leonor? Ah, yes, Leonor. Well, no doubt you have heard her sing tonight?'

Reynaud nodded. Would that he had not. Her image, and the sound of her low, melodious voice, remained indelibly stamped on his heart.

'So,' Benjamin continued. 'It is obvious, is it not? She is beautiful. Like her mother. Her music, her poems, her…' His voice trailed off, then he gazed at him with watery black eyes. 'How impressed she must be at what you have become! You were always a fine-looking boy, but as a man—*ay de mi!* The ladies must all fall in—'

Reynaud laughed. 'She was not impressed,' he said shortly.

Benjamin smiled. 'As Hassam will tell you, she is a handful. That one has a mind of her own, I fear. Also like her mother.'

'You must bear part of the blame for that, old friend,' Reynaud said with a chuckle. 'Her education was your doing.'

'And her mother's,' Benjamin amended. 'But, yes, I admit it. Since the day of her birth I have loved Leonor as if she were my own daughter. Old men grow more foolish with the years.'

Reynaud sobered. A Templar, too, could be foolish. And to be foolish was dangerous. There was no room in the life of a spy for the distraction of a woman. He would need all his wits about him in the days to come.

With a gesture, he refused the older man's offer of more wine. 'She may be in danger. Hassam fears she may be kidnapped.'

Benjamin's thin shoulders twitched. 'Kidnapped!'

'Calm yourself. I do not think that is what my uncle fears most. I think Hassam knows of some other threat in Navarre, a danger which he did not share with me.'

Benjamin quailed. 'Danger? What kind of danger?'

'I know not, at the moment. I mean not to offend you, old friend, but I am suspicious of Leonor.'

At Benjamin's thoughtful nod, Reynaud pressed the issue a step further. '"Know you the silver swan" is a coded message. She sang those very words in the hall just now.'

The old man's head snapped up. 'Coded message?'

'Ben, is it possible that Leonor could be a spy?'

'What? *Leonor?*' The old man's black eyes blazed. 'Have you left your wits in Acre? Think, man. She is a woman! At the moment, bent on being a minstrel. Is that not worrisome enough?'

Reynaud laid his forefinger against his old tutor's lips. 'We shall keep silence, then, you and I. I will protect her.'

Benjamin hugged him hard. 'Guard her well, my son.'

Reynaud knew the links of chainmail under his surcoat pressed into the old man's flesh, but the strength of Ben's embrace did not falter. Again he had to smile. In addition to Leonor, Benjamin loved him as well.

* * *

Reynaud re-entered the great hall just as the servants were clearing the tables and pushing them back against the walls to make space for dancing. Pages bustled between kitchen and scullery, folding the stained linen cloths and tossing scraps of meat to the hounds as they passed. The wine server made his rounds, collecting the cups and pitchers. Out of the corner of his eye, he saw the portly man glance about, then surreptitiously gulp the dregs from a pewter cup left on the table.

His own mouth felt dry. Just as the red-faced wine server reached for Reynaud's cup, he rescued it and downed the contents in two swallows. Then he turned to search for Leonor.

He surveyed the hall, watched as a troupe of musicians tumbled in through a doorway, one carrying a gut-strung rebec and a vielle, three others with wooden flutes, a gittern and a battered tabor drum. They took up positions at one end of the hall, and the chattering crowd cleared the floor. The string players adjusted their tuning and knights and ladies linked hands for a circle dance.

He scanned the faces of the onlookers, then searched for Leonor among the dancers, but the slim, black-haired woman in emerald silk was not among them. Surely she would not retire this early, not after such a triumphant reception? Unless...

A thread of alarm travelled up his spine. Was she in danger? He grabbed a sloshing pitcher out of the wine server's grasp and refilled his cup with a hand that trembled.

Before he could lift the wine to his lips, a low voice spoke at his elbow. 'Reynaud, do you dance this evening? Or…' Leonor looked pointedly at the wine cup in his hand '…do you prefer to drink?'

He started so violently a bit of wine spilled over the edge of his cup and wet his fingers. She moved like a cat! Her green silk tunic was girdled with gold links, accentuating the curve of her waist and hips. He worked to keep his gaze elsewhere.

'I did not see you approach.'

The grey eyes rested briefly on his, an expression of amusement in their depths. 'I did not intend you to.'

Reynaud drew in a careful breath. He was supposed to watch *her,* not the other way around. His belly tightened. She could appear and disappear like a wraith. Hassam was right—he would need all his wits to keep track of her. At this moment, the idea did not displease him as much as it should.

'Do you dance, Reynaud?' Leonor repeated.

The thought of touching her, even linking hands, brought the blood to his brain. His senses came alive, then careened out of control. He could not risk it.

'I can dance, yes. I choose not to.'

'As you wish.' She smiled up at him and his heart lurched.

He did not wish. He wanted to hold her close, drink in her scent and let his mouth explore hers.

This was madness! Was he not a holy knight?

Never had he wanted a woman so. But now his mind reeled as if he were fevered.

'You have not yet told me,' she murmured, 'which of my three songs you found most enjoyable.'

Reynaud could not answer. Here in this noisy hall was neither the place nor the time to question her about the coded words.

Count Henri approached, and she stepped to one side to accept her uncle's invitation to join the dancing. Without a backwards glance she glided away on the count's arm, pivoted and made a deep reverence.

Reynaud watched her move gracefully in the circle of dancers until his eyes burned. No wonder Benjamin was enamored. Leonor was like no other woman he had ever encountered. By the time this evening ended, every man in the hall would be in love with her. Watching over her, wanting her, was pure torture.

And suddenly he knew he could not do it.

Chapter Seven

Leonor smiled at her uncle, hoping he would not notice she had again missed a step. Guided by the rhythm of the beaten tabor, she quickly shifted from her left to her right foot and caught up. Keep count! she reminded herself. If she could not think clearly, at least she could keep track of the beats.

But she found herself ignoring both the pattern of the steps and her uncle's rambling conversation as her gaze roamed about the hall. Servants scurried in and out of the kitchen; ladies on the sidelines, gowned in gay silks and sarsenet, nodded their heads together as they gossiped. Her uncle's knights and the nobles of his court, dressed in richly embroidered tunics, argued about horses and tournaments.

And then there was Reynaud. Tall and dark-haired, he stood near the wall, his raised foot resting on a bench, talking with Aunt Alais and another lady garbed in grey silk. A wine cup rested in his hand. As she watched, he raised it to his lips.

Over the coiffed heads of the two women his eyes scanned the hall as if casually viewing his surroundings. In the next moment his glance locked with hers, and her heart stopped. He had been searching for her!

'My dear niece, you are counting under your breath,' her uncle whispered.

'Your pardon, Uncle.' She closed her eyes to shut out Reynaud's penetrating gaze from across the hall, struggled to concentrate on the count's continuing tale of a ship bound for Cyprus. When she opened her lids again, Reynaud had disappeared.

Just as suddenly he appeared at her side, his sea-green eyes burning. Without a word, he disengaged her hand from her uncle's and took his place beside her.

'That's the way, my boy.' Count Henri clapped Reynaud on the back. 'Claim her, and welcome.' Chuckling, he headed back to the head table and his wife.

Reynaud's throat felt thick and hot. 'My lady?'

'My lord, I thought you would not dance?'

'So I thought also.'

Her eyes shone with amusement. 'And now?'

Now? In truth he could not bear to watch another man—even her uncle—lay his hand on her. Now, for a few stolen moments, he would dance with her. Touch her. *Ask her about the message.*

He looked down into her eyes and she fell silent until the droning of the rebec ceased and the dance ended. Reynaud lowered their clasped fingers until they stood facing each other, jostled by retreating dancers. Slowly he drew her into the protective shadows of the far wall.

He closed her hand in his and held it down, near his thigh. In silence he twined his fingers in hers and gently tucked her arm behind her back. Unable to help himself, he drew her towards him.

What was he doing?

He had but two choices. He could hold her in his arms, as he ached to do, or he could walk away.

'Reynaud,' she said quietly, 'you are hurting my hand.' Instantly he disengaged his fingers from hers and slid his hand up to encircle her wrist. 'Your pardon. Being close to you is…difficult.'

'Then,' she questioned gently, 'why do you not release me?'

He could tell she was smiling, though he could not bring himself to look into her face. He could not answer over the hot ache in his throat. He swallowed hard and tightened his hand about her slim wrist. 'I fear you are in danger, though you may not be aware of it.'

Her eyes flared. 'I am aware. I sought it.'

'Then have a care, Leonor. Trust no one.'

She hesitated half a heartbeat, and a soft light kindled deep within her grey eyes. 'Not even you, Reynaud?'

He pressed his arm across her back, lowered his head to hers and spoke near her ear. 'Hear me, Leonor. I fear for you.' *And God help me, I fear for myself when you are near.*

'You need not fear,' she said with a laugh. 'You are a Templar. And my cousin. I would trust you with my life.'

'Then,' he whispered, 'you are indeed foolish.'

Her smile faded. 'Ah, no. I think not,' she said quietly. 'You are the friend of my childhood, Rey. I know you disapprove of what I do, but you are still my friend, are you not?'

'I am that,' he said, his voice rough with emotion. As a Templar, he could never be more than her friend. He opened his lips to ask about the words of her song, but Henri appeared and whisked her off again. He waited an hour, but she did not return.

At supper the next evening Reynaud sat curling his finger around the base of his wine cup until his knuckles ached. Another of Count Henri's snail-paced evening meals, and still Leonor had not made an appearance. He had glimpsed her earlier in the day, walking in the south garden with Benjamin, their heads bent together. He wondered what they had been discussing so intently. He had tried to find her that afternoon, to no avail. If she were indeed the messenger from his Grand Master, he would need to find out from her where he was to deliver his Templar gold.

Why was she not present at the evening meal?

Benjamin was also nowhere to be seen. That did not surprise him; except in Granada, few Jews, even respected scholars, mingled with the dinner guests in a Christian household. But neither was Benjamin's bony black-robed form visible in the assortment of servants, pages and peasants crowding against the far wall, waiting for the leavings of gravy-sopped bread and meat scraps.

The words of the conversation on either side of him buzzed in his head like swarming bees. Benjamin could take care of himself, could make himself inconspicuous as an ant if need be. But Leonor?

Never. She was far too noticeable with that mass of black hair and those large grey eyes. The scent of her hair, sweet roses with a hint of sandalwood, tormented him. He inhaled slowly, struggling to still the hammering of his heart.

'What say you, Templar?' the count shouted over the clank of cups and the din of laughter. 'Can the Christian *Reconquista* succeed against the infidel in Spain?'

Reynaud unclenched his fingers and took a deep swallow of his wine before answering. 'Your son Bernard yet fights against the Saracen. Have you never wondered why?'

The count leaned towards him. 'My son is a Hospitaller. Wherever he is, he will not rest until the infidel is vanquished, in both the Holy Land and in Spain.'

'God's mercy on you, then, Henri, for he will be absent from you for a long time. It will not be a simple victory in Jerusalem or in Spain.'

The count's bushy grey eyebrows arched upwards. 'Oh?'

Reynaud directed his gaze straight into the older

man's hazel eyes. 'It is an easy matter to take a castle, even an entire city. It is not so easy to reconquer a people. Spain has been home to both Christian and Saracen ever since the Arabs wrested the land from the Roman Goths four hundred years ago.'

'You do not hate them, the Saracen?'

'A few, aye. Most, I respect. Some—my uncle Hassam in Granada for one—I hold dear.'

Just then Leonor appeared in the doorway, clothed in a silk gown the colour of sapphires, the wide crimson-lined sleeves brushing the floor at her feet. A lanky squire at her side carried her harp. She looked like a queen. A suffocating warmth filled his chest and he struggled to control his ragged breathing. Even if he could steel himself to look upon her, he was not sure he could bear to hear her sing again.

But if she was in fact the agent he was to meet, he must identify himself to her tonight.

Across the hall their gazes met and held, and in her soft grey eyes he read a question. Under his surcoat his heart jumped erratically. *What question?*

She glided to the centre of the hall, the squire trailing behind, then lifted the carved instrument from the boy's hands and sent him a smile of gratitude. Conversation in the hall faded to a hush.

Blushing crimson, the youth backed into a seated knight, nearly overbalancing them both. The knight righted the stammering squire and clapped him on the back. 'In love now, are you, Galeran? Well, perhaps it's time. Might as well learn about heartbreak when you're young.'

Leonor waited until the squire had fled and the guffaws died down, then seated herself, detached her tuning key from the gold chain at her waist, and bent her head over the strings. She plucked softly, and when she was satisfied, she set the harp aside and rose to make a polite reverence to Lady Alais and Count Henri.

Again her glance locked with Reynaud's. Against his will, he held her eyes until his skittering pulse sounded in his ears. At last, she sent him a slow smile, and his senses exploded.

His body burned with longing, and he closed his eyes to control the tightness in his loins. In all his thirty-two years he had never seen such a beautiful woman. Poor Galeran. He knew exactly how the youth suffered.

She began her song and Reynaud gulped a mouthful of wine. If she *was* the agent sent to meet him, she would again sing of the silver swan. And if she did, he must find a way to answer with the second half of the coded message.

He motioned to the wine server to refill his cup. Mesmerised, he watched Leonor's slim form move subtly with the music, drinking in every nuance in her voice, the rich poetry of the verse.

She began a second verse. Her voice floated over the melody echoed by the harp, and suddenly the words smacked into his brain. *Know you the silver swan?*

He sucked in his breath.

Over the edge of his wine cup he glimpsed a

movement at the back of the hall. A black-cloaked figure stopped, then crept forwards again, advancing step by step like a cat. Closer, now. A few arm-lengths more and he would be able to make out the man's features hidden under the loose hood.

The stranger's hard blue eyes studied the throng of listeners, then peered at Leonor. She drew the song to a close and raised her head expectantly, her hands poised over the harp strings.

An odd silence descended over the hall. No one moved. No one so much as coughed or cleared his throat. The silence stretched until the humming in his brain set his teeth on edge.

It must be now. Answer with the correct response. He should have spoken before, but he could not bring himself to believe Leonor was involved. Now, hearing the words for the second time in two nights, there was no mistaking it.

Still, he hesitated.

He must speak. As soon as she delivered the message to him, her task would be complete and she would be safe. Then he could leave Moyanne, leave Leonor in the protection of her uncle, and ride away from the sweet torture he endured every minute he was in her presence. Every league he put between them drew the danger away from her.

He opened his mouth, but before he could get a word out, a gruff voice spoke from the shadows.

'The silver swan, lady? It sings but once, then dies.'

Reynaud froze, an icy hand clamping his spine. That was the correct response. But who...?

Leonor sat without moving, her eyes on the stranger. A pulse throbbed at her throat.

Reynaud swung his gaze away from her to see the unknown speaker's face.

Chapter Eight

A burly, sandy-haired man with a short, grey-streaked beard and ice-blue eyes stepped out of the shadows and stalked towards Leonor. An ankle-length tunic of dun-coloured linen showed beneath a fine overrobe of red damask trimmed in fur too heavy for the warm, stuffy Moyanne summer.

Reynaud's gut tightened. He rose from his place at the head table and strode towards Leonor, still seated in the centre of the hall. A rustle of whispers accompanied his every step.

The stranger approached from the opposite direction. 'My lady, I would speak with you. In private.'

Leonor turned an assessing gaze on the man. 'About what, my lord?'

Reynaud winced at her directness, but marvelled that her voice sounded so calm. Only the fluttering pulse in her throat betrayed her unease.

'The words you sang just now,' the man said in an undertone, 'offer one part of a puzzle. I present its mate. I believe you have something more to tell me?'

She opened her lips to reply just as Reynaud reached her side.

'Do not,' he said in a voice intended for her ears alone. 'Tell him nothing, Leonor. This man is false.'

Leonor's eyes widened. 'But he answered—'

Reynaud closed his hand over her shoulder. 'Please, Leonor, say nothing. Trust me!'

'Nay, lady,' the stranger interjected softly. 'Trust *me*! This Templar—' he spat the word in Reynaud's direction '—is the one who is false.'

Leonor remained silent for a long moment. 'You are not known to me, my lord.' She looked up at the man with cool, grey eyes. 'And so I would have your name, if you please.'

The stranger drew himself up and bowed. 'I am Bernard de Rodez. Count Henri's son.'

Onlookers gasped, and a babble of voices rose. Count Henri, his face pasty, bolted from his chair and clutched the table edge. The buzz of whispered questions rose and ebbed around them like restless waves in the sea.

Reynaud felt his world tilt. The count's son? Bernard of Moyanne was Bernard de Rodez?

'And you, Templar?' Leonor said, her voice low.

'You know who I am. Your cousin, Reynaud.'

A light flared in the stranger's blue eyes. 'Only "Reynaud"? Nothing more? Reynaud of…what?'

Reynaud blinked. He levelled his gaze on the

count's son and stepped in close. Keeping his eyes on the stranger's mottled face, he measured out his words. 'I am bastard-born,' he said quietly.

Bernard de Rodez's pale eyes did not blink. 'A touching story,' he sneered. 'You are not landed, then. Or titled.'

'True,' Reynaud said. 'I know not who my father was.' He let out a long breath. He did not like this man.

'A landless bastard parading in Templar robes would certainly lie to gain information,' de Rodez growled. 'And a fortune in gold as well.'

'That is false,' Reynaud replied quietly.

De Rodez snorted and dropped his voice even lower. 'I can prove my identity by merely calling out to my father.' He waved a thick arm towards Count Henri, who clung, frozen, to the trestle table. 'But you? You have no way to prove who you are.'

'That, too, is false,' Reynaud said. The chatter of voices began to swirl around them, like the clacking of geese.

De Rodez planted his feet apart, caressing his sword hilt with blunt fingers. 'Well, then? Shall you prove your claim by force of arms?'

Reynaud chuckled. 'You will not succeed in goading me into swordplay. The man who strikes such a blow has run out of ideas. And that, I have not.'

At Leonor's questioning look, he smiled. 'Say nothing to this man, Leonor.'

Her eyes rounded. 'But he gave the proper response.'

'As would I, had I been given the chance.'

She looked from one to the other, her face stricken. 'One of you is lying.'

'True,' Reynaud said. Then he bent and put his lips to her ear. 'I venture that your father did not know of your…*other* mission, for Emir Yusef.'

Bernard de Rodez jiggled his sword hilt. 'What is all this whispering?' he shouted over the mounting noise around them. Suddenly he surged forwards and seized Leonor's forearm. 'You, lady! Come with me!'

Instantly an expectant hush fell over the hall.

From under her heavy lashes, Leonor gave the burly man a long look. 'If, my lord, you are indeed my Uncle Henri's son, then I am your cousin by marriage. And, Cousin, while I do not question your heritage, I do reserve the right to make my own decision about where I go and with whom. And about two men who now present themselves in the same role.'

Reynaud stared at her. *Hassam, I see now why you treasure her so. She is brave and quick and impossible, all at the same time. There is none to match her in all the world.*

'Lea, you must trust me,' he murmured. 'Not this man, no matter who he claims to be. Your message is intended for me.'

Leonor gave a little moan and broke free of de Rodez's grasp. For an interminable minute her grey eyes probed first de Rodez and then himself. At last she gave a tiny shake of her head and shrugged. 'I trust neither of you.'

She moved to face Reynaud, close enough that he caught her scent of roses and the dusky spice of sandalwood. He drew back, his heart hammering. She must not trust de Rodez! If she did her life could be in danger.

De Rodez pivoted away from her with a snort of disgust.

In that instant Leonor reached out, cupped Reynaud's face in her hands and drew his head down to hers. Her breath fluttered in his ear as she whispered three words.

'Tonight. Trust me.'

Count Henri lurched forwards and laid a shaking hand on Bernard de Rodez's shoulder, then clasped his thin arms around the stocky knight. 'My son! My son!'

'Father.' The gruff voice was cool. Detached.

Leonor wondered at the stranger. He did not remove his hand from the well-worn sword hilt; neither did he return the count's embrace. Was he indeed Henri's heir? After a separation of close to thirty summers, as Aunt Alais had told her, how could the two men recognise one another?

'Bernard,' her uncle choked out. 'I knew you would come some day, I knew it. Just the other day I was telling Alais— Oh! But you do not yet know Alais, my wife. After your mother died…'

The old man's voice faltered.

'You remarried,' Bernard de Rodez finished for him. 'Are there children? Other heirs?'

'No,' Henri replied. 'I have no son but you, and now you have returned at last. I thought I should not live to see—'

'I do not stay, Father. I have business in Spain, and then I return to the Holy Land.'

'Not stay? But surely…' The glow in her uncle's lined face dimmed. Leonor's heart contracted at the pain in the old man's eyes.

Reynaud turned away with a ragged indrawn breath, his shoulders hunched and tense under the Templar robe. 'The bastard,' he breathed. He clenched his fists at his side. 'The count has not seen his son since boyhood. You would think—'

Leonor covered his tightly balled hand with her own. 'It is between them, Rey. Fathers and sons often hurt each other. You can do nothing.'

But she wondered at the brusque manner in which the Hospitaller de Rodez spoke to his father. His words were cruel. She shot a glance at Reynaud's strained face, watched his nostrils flare as he struggled with his own emotions. Trembling with anger barely kept in check, he shook his head.

Count Henri made a motion to draw his son off to one side of the hall, but de Rodez resisted. Deliberately the stone-faced knight reached down with one hand and plucked his father's fingers from his arm. Then he pivoted and his gravelly voice addressed her.

'Madam, I would speak with you. In private.' He strode to her side and gripped her arm above the elbow, squeezing her flesh until she bit her lip to keep from crying out. 'Come,' he muttered.

An arrow of fear pierced her belly, but she managed to keep her voice even. 'Very well, my lord,' she replied. 'Since you insist.'

She flashed a look at Reynaud, sending him a silent message with her eyes. *Trust me.* Then, without a backwards glance she tugged her arm free and moved towards the doorway, Bernard de Rodez breathing audibly at her heels.

She paused in the outer corridor, but de Rodez prodded her up the circular stone stairway to the castle rooftop. Guards were posted along the rampart, and she resolved to speak with her cousin de Rodez only within their sight.

She reached the battlement and turned to face him.

A shaking hand pressed Reynaud's arm. 'Come, Templar,' Count Henri said in an unsteady voice. 'Drink with me.'

Reynaud reached an arm around the older man's shoulders. He prayed that Leonor would trust him, and not de Rodez. At least he hoped she would not give the message to the Hospitaller. Slowly he guided Henri back to the high table, where he lowered the count on to the wooden chair, and settled himself beside the trembling man.

Henri sat motionless, his face naked with anguish. A hand of iron closed around Reynaud's heart. Bernard de Rodez did not know how fortunate he was to *have* a father. A father who welcomed him home. A father who loved him. He clamped his jaw shut until it ached. Count Henri did not deserve such treatment.

And Leonor! He stared at the doorway through which she had disappeared with de Rodez. What mischief was she up to? With a groan, he hailed the hovering wine server and lifted the pitcher out of his hands.

The man blinked. 'Do you desire aught else, sir knight?'

'No,' Reynaud growled. He sloshed the liquid into Henri's cup, then filled his own. The thought of Leonor and Henri's son together made his blood run cold.

He turned to the count and raised his drinking vessel. 'To families,' he said, his tone dry. He downed the entire cup in three gulps and poured it full again.

Count Henri sighed. 'It is understandable, my friend. What man would not prefer to spend time with a beautiful young woman instead of an old—' His voice cracked. 'Let us drink to something more constant.' He lifted his cup. 'To wine,' the count proposed. 'A God-given elixir for…' his voice faltered '…easing heartache.'

'To wine!' Reynaud echoed. He tipped his cup and drank deeply, savouring the heady, fruity flavor of the crimson liquid. Over the rim of his cup he directed a glance at the count.

The older man's gaze slid away, but not before Reynaud had glimpsed the shiny tears brimming in his hazel eyes.

'Wine bearer!' Reynaud shouted, his voice unexpectedly hoarse. 'Bring us another pitcher!'

Chapter Nine

Leonor faced Bernard de Rodez, careful to stay within sight of the two men-at-arms keeping watch from the castle rampart. A chilly breeze blew across the rooftop, and she shivered.

'You wished to speak with me?'

De Rodez seized her wrist. 'Tell me, lady,' he gritted out. 'Now!'

Leonor drew in a long breath, willing her voice to remain calm. 'Unhand me. I can tell you nothing if the guards…' she inclined her head towards the two men pacing to and fro along the wall walk '…throw you in my uncle's dungeon for assaulting me. And if you do not release me, I will call them to do just that.'

De Rodez swore and loosened his fingers. Deftly, Leonor stepped back, out of his grasp. 'Explain yourself, sir, and be brief. I have duties elsewhere.'

De Rodez's eyes glittered. 'I would know the message you carry from Emir Yusef of Granada.'

Leonor stared at the scowling man who stood before her. Cold blue eyes, so emotionless they looked like polished stone, gazed back at her from under shaggy, sand-coloured eyebrows. His thin lips pursed as he awaited her answer.

Her stomach churned. Was this man indeed the intended recipient of Yusef's message? Not Reynaud? Yusef himself had not known the identity of the recipient, else the emir would have communicated the information to Reynaud before they left Granada.

'Answer me!' de Rodez demanded. 'And be quick about it.' Her heart began to pound with a sick apprehension. Why had Reynaud spoken against this man, warned her not to trust him? Was de Rodez an imposter? Perhaps even a spy for the enemies of Granada's emir?

Or was it Reynaud who was false?

The hard, unblinking eyes bored into hers. She shivered and suddenly her mind cleared. It mattered not whether Reynaud and Bernard de Rodez were allies or enemies. She had a message to deliver.

De Rodez grated his thumbnail back and forth on his sword hilt. 'Lady, I grow impatient!'

For a long moment she studied the leather-booted feet planted before her. At last she raised her gaze to meet his. She would do what she must.

She nodded once. De Rodez grunted, then inclined his head towards her.

Quickly she spoke a few words in a low voice.

* * *

A plump serving maid sped past Reynaud, a steaming cup of spiced wine and some bread and cheese on a tray. He ducked back into the curtained recess cut in the stone wall and within minutes the girl hurried back along the passageway and disappeared down the staircase.

He breathed a sigh of relief. The other castle inhabitants lay sleeping, nobles within assigned private chambers, visiting knights and men-at-arms sprawled on pallets in the great hall. But a faint light shone under Leonor's door.

Good. She was yet awake. She had much to answer for. He tapped softly on the heavy oak door.

The silence lengthened until he swore he could hear his own heartbeat. His head ached from the wine.

He tapped again.

The door cracked open, then swung inwards on its leather hinges. Leonor stood before him, the flickering candle in her hand sending shadows dancing into the corners of the tiny chamber. Before he could speak, she blew out the flame, plunging the room into inky blackness.

'Reynaud,' she whispered. 'I thought you would never come.'

'The devil himself could not keep me away,' he said, keeping his voice low. He reached out and closed his hand around her forearm. 'Though once this matter is finished, you may wish I had not come.'

She gasped and he tightened his grip until he could feel the slender bone under his fingers. Fury danced like hot coals in his veins. An hour ago he and Count Henri had watched in astonishment when Bernard de Rodez strode across the great hall and bid his father a curt farewell. An urgent matter pressed, he said. His horse was saddled and ready in the bailey; he would ride south this very night.

At that moment Reynaud knew Leonor had betrayed him, given the secret message to de Rodez instead of himself. Now he pinned her in a grip that would leave bruises. 'Who sent you?' he growled into the dark. 'Answer me, damn you!'

'I am sent by Yusef, Emir of Granada.' The cool voice spoke just below his chin, her breath fanning his throat.

He stifled a groan. He did not know whether he wanted to kill her or ravish her. His cousin, his Leonor, had become his enemy.

'You took the word of a false knight over mine? Why?' he demanded. Anguish made his voice harsh. 'And the message you gave him? What was it?'

'None.'

'You lie, Leonor. De Rodez rode out of the bailey scarce an hour ago, pleading "urgent business". Your uncle is sick with grief. And I…' He paused, feeling himself teeter on the brink of madness.

He yanked hard on her arm, pulling her forwards against his chest. 'I could kill you with my bare hands for what you have done.'

Leonor said nothing. She stood motionless, her

head tucked under his chin, her soft, warm body pressed against his. He inhaled the spicy-sweet scent of her hair and something inside him snapped.

'Leonor, why did you do it?'

'I did nothing, Reynaud.'

'Nothing! Again you lie!'

'Nothing,' her low voice repeated.

Reynaud gave a short laugh. 'Where, then, did Bernard de Rodez thunder off to?'

'Where I sent him,' Leonor replied, her tone cool. 'Now, Rey, if you will release me…'

She stepped away from him, and in the next moment he heard the burr of wooden rings and the swish of a curtain being drawn aside. Moonlight spilled through the narrow-paned window, washing the chamber with silvery blue light.

She moved to a table, lifted the goblet of wine, and sipped from it. Then she held the cup out to him.

'No. I have drunk too much already on your account this night.'

Leonor sighed. 'Drink it, Rey,' she ordered in a quiet voice. 'You will need it when I tell you what I have done.'

He pushed aside the wine cup. 'What, exactly, is it you have done?' he said, his voice tight.

'I told de Rodez where to travel.'

He stared at Leonor in disbelief. 'Repeat that,' he demanded. 'You told de Rodez *what*?'

Leonor glanced up from the small table where she was wrapping the last of the bread and cheese in an oiled cloth. 'I told him to ride south, to Saragossa.

There he was to seek one Ramiro, at the house of
Miguel de Alvaro.'

Reyaud's equilibrium wobbled once again. 'You
sent him to the Templars' secret holding?' He paced
the length of the small chamber, anger coiling in his
belly. 'This matter is not some child's game.' He
spat the words at her. 'The fate of Granada hangs in
the balance. My God-given mission is to prevent the
bloodbath that is to come.'

'Of course,' Leonor replied, her voice matter of
fact. She moved to the carved oak chest in the far
corner of the chamber and lifted the lid, propping it
against the stone wall.

'And I intend to help you. So naturally I sent de
Rodez south.' She sent him a long look. '*We* are
riding north.'

'North?' Again he paced to the far wall and back.
'By all the saints, who is "we"?' In the dim light he
watched her lips purse in exasperation.

'North,' she repeated. 'Then east, to Carcassonne.
Unless,' she continued, her voice taking on a slight
edge, 'you are not, after all, the secret recipient I was
sent to meet?'

She turned her back and bent over the open chest,
tugged out a length of white fabric and tossed it on
to the bed. 'You and I, Rey,' she said over her
shoulder as she rummaged in the chest once more.

'You and I *what*?' he growled.

'I am coming with you. To Carcassonne.'

He almost choked. 'Never!'

She flung out another garment, a cloak he

gathered from the way it sailed past him and settled like a shroud over the bed. Again she dove into the depths of the chest, and when she spoke her voice was muffled.

'How soon will you be ready to leave?'

Reynaud stiffened. '*I* will ride now, before this night grows one hour older.'

'As will I.' Leonor straightened to face him, planting both hands on her hips. 'At this very moment Galeran the squire waits in the bailey with my saddled mare. I have already taken leave of Aunt Alais. Benjamin and I made our farewells before supper. He was not pleased, poor man, but I—'

'Talked him into it,' Reynaud finished for her. 'I cannot imagine what tale you told him.'

'No tale but the truth, that I ride with you to further try my skill as a troubadour. You, of course…' she leveled an odd look at him, curiosity mixed with something else. Respect? '…have other business there.'

'That I do, lady,' he growled. 'And I do not take you with me. It is not safe.' How could he stand being near her day and night, watching her, worrying over her safety? *Aching to touch her.* His throat tightened.

'You must take me,' Leonor said quietly. 'You promised my father you would protect me. You cannot leave me here in Moyanne. Bernard de Rodez is sure to return to take vengeance for the goose chase I have sent him on.'

Without another word, she bent over the bed

and began rolling the garments she had collected into a bundle.

Reynaud's gut knotted. She was right. He could not leave her here unprotected.

He watched her secure the bundle with a leather thong and for the first time noted with a start what she was wearing. Not a silk gown, but a worn-looking forest-green linen tunic extended below her knees, split up the sides for riding. Underneath that a peasant's cross-wrapped leggings covered her legs. She had coiled her hair up under a floppy cap of much-washed wool.

She stood waiting, the roll of clothing under one arm and the package of food under the other. 'You had better have more of the wine, Rey. Your face is pale as a ghost.'

He jerked in barely suppressed fury. 'By the saints, I feel like no ghost. More like a dragon!'

'That,' Leonor said with a hiccup of laughter, 'is obvious. Ghosts are silent!'

Fear and anger pounded through his body. 'Carcassonne is a hotbed of Christian heresy and rampaging, landless knights. It is no place for an unworldly maid.'

And now he knew it was also close to the secret headquarters of the Templars. He had urgent, dangerous business there, about which she knew nothing.

'Come,' she whispered. 'We have not a moment to lose. It is only a matter of time before de Rodez realises the trick I have played.'

Reynaud studied the young woman who stood re-

solutely before him. 'Who is this Ramiro in Saragossa?' he snapped.

'Ramiro?' The moon's silvery light played over
her face, highlighting the high cheekbones, the full,
downturned lips, the delicate skin visible through
the opening at the neck of her tunic. She looked for
all the world like a chess player who had just
trounced her opponent.

'I know not. There must a hundred Ramiros in
Saragossa. I thought to keep de Rodez busy for a
time.'

He stared at her. She was a djinn. And God knew
he was caught in her thrall. Nay, not just caught.
Drowning. This innocent creature, so enthralled with
the outside world, could not possibly guess the peril
she rushed towards.

Or the peril she presented to his immortal soul.

With an oath he turned away. The thought of
Leonor as his constant companion day and night
made him light-headed. It was both joy and agony
to be near her.

But so be it. There was no other choice; he must
take her with him.

He bowed his head. He could never assuage the
hunger of his spirit. But until his last breath, he
would fight the dark pull of desire she seeded in
him.

The squire Galeran gripped the mare's bit in his
left hand as he struggled to control the restive grey
stallion the Templar had left in his care. 'Quiet, now,'

he whispered at the huge beast. 'Thy master would not like it if you bit me.'

And, the boy groaned inwardly, would not pay him one denier if his horse were abused. 'But,' he muttered, eyeing the destrier with suspicion, ''tis tempting.'

In truth, the huge animal frightened him. Never had he seen so fine a mount, and caparisoned in white silk with a cross of scarlet samite stitched on each side. A handsome coat for such a horse!

Galeran drew off the silk trapper, folded it, and tied it behind the saddle, as the lady Leonor had ordered. If he lived to be as old as his Uncle Henri, he would never understand a woman. Not even in Carcassonne, at his father's castle, did a knight's mount go uncoated. Such a covering announced at a glance one's heritage as well as one's allegiance.

Galeran sighed. If *he* were skilled enough to be a Templar knight, the most respected, the most coveted of military orders, he would not hesitate to proclaim it to the world.

He led the stallion and the lady Leonor's mare to a shadowed corner of the outer courtyard and settled down to wait.

If *he* were a Templar, just think how his companions in training at Moyanne would look up to him. And the ladies! His heartbeat quickened. All the ladies would admire him, would beg him to wear their favours in the lists. Would—

Ladies! What ladies? Was he dreaming? A Templar had naught to do with ladies. A Templar pledged his spirit and his body to God. A Templar was… Galeran groaned aloud with the realisation.

Chaste.

How did they stand it? Even now, at the thought of the lady Leonor, his body flushed with a strange heat. She had the most beautiful voice, the most exquisite breasts.

An owl hooted from the woods just across the drawbridge. The stallion tossed his mighty head and stepped backwards, jerking Galeran off balance. He stumbled and his toe stubbed against a protruding paving stone. He swore his most manly oath.

A low, lilting voice came from the shadows. 'What, Galeran, are you not pleased by your task?'

The lady Leonor emerged from the narrow gateway and Galeran's body went cold, then hot.

'I—I wrapped your harp safe in a carpet, and I tied rags around the horses' hooves, just as you directed, my lady.'

Lady Leonor stepped across the bailey and approached so close he could smell her perfume. 'Thank you, Galeran. None should hear of our departure. Nor,' she added, sending him a penetrating look, 'should anyone know the direction in which we travel.'

'Oh, aye, my lady. I swear none shall know it from my lips.'

She smiled at him and suddenly his lungs refused to take breath in or out.

'Come, help me to mount. I must be ready the moment Lord Reynaud appears.'

'Aye, my lady,' he choked out. He released the grey stallion's bit, laced his fingers together and cupped both hands for her tiny foot.

'And, Galeran,' she murmured as she settled herself on the cream mare's back, 'if you do not mention to Reynaud that you have been waiting here with our horses since suppertime, I will be in your debt.'

Galeran grinned down at his throbbing toe. The thought of his beautiful lady being in his debt made his head spin. He would do anything for her. Anything.

The Templar strode through the gate, a bundle under one arm, and Galeran suddenly recalled his duties. The knight gave a sharp whistle, and when the destrier ambled up, he nestled the bundle under the cantle, stepped into the stirrup and swung himself into the saddle. The knight turned the horse to face Galeran, leaned down and pressed a coin into his palm.

'My thanks, lad. That's for your service. And this…' a second coin clinked against the first '…is for your silence.'

Galeran nodded. 'Yes, my lord. I understand.' His heart nearly burst with pride. He had done his duty, and he had been richly rewarded.

The Templar stepped his destrier forwards, towards the drawbridge which had not yet been raised for the night. He dropped another coin into the gnarled hand of the old man huddled beside the iron-toothed winch, and Galeran heard some mumbled words of thanks. Then the knight rode out of the castle yard and over the bridge, the sound of the horse's hooves muffled.

The lady Leonor stepped her mare after the stallion, then drew up the reins and leaned forwards, reaching her hand down to clasp Galeran's. 'You have done admirably, Galeran. Fare you well.' She pressed his fingers lightly and was gone.

The squire brought his hand to his nostrils and sniffed at the elusive sweet scent of her skin. Indeed, he had been more than richly rewarded this night.

Ah, perhaps he would not be a Templar after all.

Chapter Ten

The two horses moved through the shadowy trees like wraiths, milk-pale in the moonlight. An owl called as they passed under a grey willow tree, and the hair on Leonor's neck prickled. It was too quiet.

Reynaud reined in ahead of her and pointed in silence to the east, away from the village of Moyanne. Her heart hammering, she nodded and they stepped their mounts forwards.

Suddenly she was frightened. *What was she doing, riding away with Reynaud to God knew what?* It had seemed a simple task at the time, carrying a message for someone unknown even to Emir Yusef. All she had to do was sing a particular song, wait for the proper response, and pass a message to the contact. She had not expected the contact to be her cousin Reynaud.

But then she had no choice. Some instinct told her not to trust Bernard de Rodez, even though he was

Uncle Henri's son; she'd decided to trust Reynaud. Now that she had thrown in her lot with the Templar knight, a knife edge of uncertainty sliced at her belly. She knew this was more than a simple excursion to Carcassonne. There was more at stake, and she was embroiled in it up to her neck. Reynaud was on some kind of a mission and he had enemies who wanted to stop him.

Until this moment she had not clearly understood that she could be in real danger. Still, she was with Reynaud. All she had to do was stay close to the dark figure ahead of her and he would keep her safe.

Behind her a branch snapped. Instantly Reynaud glanced back, his face pale as an egg in the gauzy light. He waited until she drew abreast of him, then raised his hand, signalling for silence. He cocked his head, listening intently, then gestured for her to leave the pilgrim road and follow him into the trees.

All she could hear was her own laboured breathing, and the more she tried to inhale and exhale quietly, the louder it seemed. Her heartbeat thudded in her ears.

Another owl screeched over her head, then cut its cry short and flapped off. Something had startled it. Before she could draw breath she heard hooves pounding along the road. Had de Rodez discovered her ruse so soon?

Reynaud held up his forefinger. One rider. He backed his mount further into the trees, and Leonor grasped her reins so tight her fingers went numb.

The sound of the horseman drew nearer, and she

stopped breathing. The hoofbeats grew louder, louder, and then suddenly faded. A shudder rippled down her spine. Whoever it was had passed their hiding place.

They waited in silence until the trill of a night bird broke the quiet, then cautiously stepped their horses out of the trees. Without speaking they regained the pilgrim road and started forwards again.

An hour passed. When a rat scuttled across her path, Leonor cried out and Reynaud drew rein.

'What is wrong?' he hissed over his shoulder.

She hesitated. It wasn't only the startling noise of the small animal; she was suddenly seeing the obvious. There was more, much more, to the world outside Granada than she had ever imagined.

'I am wondering what I have unleashed by side-tracking that oaf Bernard de Rodez.'

'Why *now* do you think of that?'

'That man is up to something. How greedy he was for information! He wheedled and pried until I thought I would scream.'

'What else did you tell him?'

In spite of her unease, she managed to smile, but she ignored the question. 'Rey, who is Bernard de Rodez really? What does he want?'

Reynaud's head came up. 'He is a Hospitaller knight. One of others in his order who hate the idea of Granada's alliance with the Templars.' He pricked his destrier forwards. 'And he wants the Templar gold I carry.'

Her mare threaded its way along the leaf-softened

path and she studied the lean figure riding noiselessly through the low-branched trees a few paces ahead of her.

'Where do you fit in, Reynaud? Why are you carrying Templar gold in your saddlebag?'

He did not answer.

'Why will you not tell me?'

'I do not want you to know these things.'

'But why?'

'Trust me, Lea,' he growled. 'You are safer not knowing.'

For an instant her heart stopped beating. It was clear he had not told her everything. He was struggling with something. But she did trust him.

'Are your loyalties to Granada and the Templar at odds? Are you pulled in two directions?'

Again he did not answer.

His face looked white and strained, his lips stretched thin, his jaw tight. The look he sent her would scorch snowflakes. But the pain in his gaze when he pinned her with those stormy green eyes kept her from questioning him further.

Goodness! What had seemed like a simple favor to Emir Yusef, and an adventure for her, was turning into something complicated and frightening. Rey was right. The world beyond Granada was dangerous.

But she would never admit her fear to *him*. Never. He would scowl at her, make her feel like a child, small and insignificant. She had revered Reynaud when they were young. Now that he was a man, she was not sure how she felt about him. As a man, he seemed aloof and forbidding. There was no joy in him.

They rode until the dawn sky turned a milky grey, then veered off the road and took shelter in a thickly tangled copse of cypress and blooming tamarisk. Reynaud dismounted and spread one of the travel carpets over the ground; Leonor draped another over a low-hanging branch to provide some shade when the sun rose.

Reynaud stared at their makeshift camp. Should he lie down to rest next to her? Sleep beside her, without touching her?

He was glad of the wine in his pack. He welcomed its numbing power, prayed it would render his body insensible to temptation. Being near her was pure agony. He had tried to mask his feelings by being curt, but that had worked only up to a point.

A sharp pain needled through his heart at the puzzled hurt in her eyes each time he bit out sharp words. Nevertheless, it kept at bay the fire that smouldered just beneath his carefully controlled exterior.

Was it enough? He sucked in a lungful of the sultry, lavender-scented air and listened to the drone of honeybees in the sheltered glade. No matter what he did, Leonor was always in his mind. Foolish she might be. Headstrong and heedless of dangers she knew nothing about. He disliked her naïvety as much as he desired her. He would protect her with his last breath.

He wrenched his gaze away from her and focused

instead on his warhorse, tied to a thick cypress branch next to Leonor's mare, and swore under his breath. How could he stand lying beside her? Smelling her hair? Feeling her warmth?

Leonor settled the wrapped bundle of bread and cheese on the carpet and motioned to him. Without speaking he knelt across from her and accepted the food she handed him, careful not to graze his fingers against hers.

They ate in silence. He drank more of the wine than he should, then pulled the chainmail shirt off over his head and stretched out on the carpet with his back to Leonor. He heard her re-wrap the food parcel and slip it back into her saddlebag. He closed his eyes, feigning sleep.

'Rey?' she whispered.

He steeled himself not to reply. With a sigh she settled herself on the opposite side of the carpet, not touching him but so close the heat of her body scorched his skin.

'Rey?' she said again. 'Are you awake?'

He worked to keep his breathing even. Every nerve in his rigid frame throbbed with wanting, as if a fire danced along his veins. It was torture to lie close to her.

He lay awake while her breathing slowed and gradually subsided into the rhythmic pattern of slumber.

Leonor wakened only once. Reynaud sat a few paces away under a drooping willow branch, staring fixedly at something beyond her head.

'Rey?'

Instantly he focused his gaze on her and his lips formed a wry smile. 'Go back to sleep, Lea. All is well.' His voice was low and rough, but his words, spoken so calmly and deliberately, soothed her. He was sharp-spoken and cynical, but he was protecting her, and for that she was grateful. She admired him for it; she knew he did not want the burden.

She woke again hours later to find him still sitting under the willow, his knees bent, his head pillowed on his folded arms.

'Rey,' she whispered. He lifted his head and looked at her with red-rimmed eyes.

'Rey, you need not sleep sitting up. Why not simply share the carpet with me?'

It took him a long minute to answer. 'I have always slept alone, even when I was a boy.'

Aye, she remembered. She remembered something else as well. With each league they covered Reynaud grew more snappish and blunt-spoken. Something was amiss.

'You resent my presence, do you not?'

Wearily, he nodded. 'But no more or less than before.'

She bit her lip hard. 'Or perhaps it is just me, myself, that you resent? A woman who plays and sings for others? A woman who does not meet your standards of behaviour?'

He sent her a long look, but said nothing.

That was it. He did not like her. Somehow the realisation made her chest hurt.

Chapter Eleven

At mid-morning, they set off again. The sun climbed high above them, a ball of merciless light in the sapphire blue summer sky. The heat pounded on Leonor's head until her temples throbbed with each step the mare took. She clamped her jaw tightly shut and urged the horse forwards over the rutted path. Dust stung her eyes, clogged her nose and throat. Pulling the white headscarf over her mouth, she glared at the rump of Reynaud's grey destrier and tried not to cough. Sweat plastered her tunic to her back.

She was hot and grimy and so sticky that buzzing tiny gnats swarmed around her, catching in her hair. Three hours ago she had laboriously brushed out the tangles and coiled it back up under the turban she wore. Oh, to have a bath! Or even splash cool water over her face.

Could Reynaud not slow his pace? Or at least rest from time to time?

'May we stop?' Leonor called.

'No.' He bit out the word.

She could curse the man. 'Rey, I am bone-weary and hot and dusty and—'

He turned his mount to face her. 'Can you not keep quiet?' he snapped.

Heat suffused her face. 'But I am thirsty.'

'So am I,' came his clipped response.

Tears stung behind her eyelids. 'Whenever I ask a question, you growl at me like an angry wolf. I would prefer Benjamin's endless grammar lessons to tiptoeing through a clutch of hen's eggs to avoid your sharp tongue.'

He reined away. 'So be it,' he called over his shoulder.

Leonor clenched her teeth until her jaw hurt. 'As a travelling companion, you are impossible!'

'That I know,' he shouted back.

She stared at his rigid back, then prodded her mount forwards until she rode beside him. 'You have changed, Rey. You are not the same person I revered as a child. Then you were merry, and you told me tales of knights in far-off places. You would even halt your training to play at hoops or teach me chess. Then,' she said with deliberation, 'you were my friend.'

'That has not changed, Lea.'

A curious flash of anger cut into her brain, and more words spilled out before she could catch them. 'And then you left Granada, rode away to France for some man's reason that did not include me. You abandoned me!'

Reynaud spurred ahead, then halted and turned his horse into her path. 'Lea, I had to go. I had to find my own place in life.'

'I wept for a whole week. I hated you!'

He frowned at her, a muscle twitching in his jaw. 'You were a child then, as was I. You are a woman now.'

A wash of rage flooded her body from neck to toe. 'What difference does that make? I am jouncing along behind you in this stifling heat and dust, and all you can do is remind me that I am a woman? That I know already!'

Reynaud leaned towards her. Heat waves shimmered around his broad shoulders and his dark un-covered head. She gulped a breath of the languid, lavender-scented air.

'You insisted on coming with me. This is what real life is like outside Granada, where you were fed iced sherbets in your shaded bower.'

'You *liked* iced sherbets! Oh, Rey, I understood you when you were a boy.'

One dark eyebrow arched. 'You were young, then.'

The man was maddening. She stared at him as if she had never seen him before. He was well made. Handsome, even, with his finely sculpted nose and mouth and those green eyes. Unexpect-edly her heart caught.

'You were also young once,' she said softly. 'I looked up to you, admired you. Now you are a man, and…and I do not understand you.' She bit her parched lower lip until she tasted blood. 'I do not know this stranger who rides before me.'

The oddest look crossed his face, and then he gave her a lopsided smile and for an instant she glimpsed regret in his eyes. 'No one knows me, Lea. Not even myself.'

'You are a Templar. A warrior for hire.'

His mouth thinned. 'That I am not. There are more important things than fighting. One is living without knowing who, or what, I am.'

Without another word he pulled hard on the reins, and the big destrier turned a circle and lumbered ahead.

They rode for another hour, then he slowed until Leonor caught up to him and he turned the grey to stand nose to nose with her cream mare.

'Are you thirsty?'

She nodded. He handed her the goatskin bag tied to his pommel. 'Drink.'

She uncorked the vessel, pulled the white face veil to one side and tipped her head back. Water dribbled out of one corner of her mouth, and Reynaud reached to retrieve the skin.

'That's enough. More, and you will be sick.'

'More, and I will no longer be athirst!' she snapped. She snatched the container out of his hand.

He closed his fingers around her wrist. 'Do not test my patience, Leonor.' He gave her arm a gentle shake, and the goatskin dropped into his open palm. 'We will stop at dusk. You may drink all you wish then.'

Her gaze followed the water skin as he recorked

it and let it drop over his saddle horn. 'I would have more now,' she countered.

'That, I know,' he said evenly. 'You do not know what is good for you.' He guided his horse ahead. 'Tonight,' he repeated, his voice low and rough. 'Now, ride. Ride until I tell you to stop.'

Leonor pressed her dry lips together. 'You spew out orders like bossy old Benjamin.'

Reynaud nodded. 'Benjamin has your welfare in mind.'

She glared at his back. 'And you?'

'I, also. Now, move.'

Reynaud glanced back over his shoulder to make sure she heeded his command. Her usually cool grey eyes were aflame. Then, as he watched, the hot, angry light in her gaze dimmed, then faded.

'You are travel-weary,' he said. 'And tomorrow it will be worse. Tomorrow we leave the pilgrim road and travel overland, through the fields and woods, to bypass Toulouse.'

'Toulouse! But why? I have always longed to see Toulouse. I could try my skill on the harp at the castle court, for I am told that Great Eleanor—'

'I am known in Toulouse,' he said shortly. 'And not welcome. Their count is, or rather was, a Hospitaller.'

His gut wrenched at the disappointment written on her face. 'I am sorry, Lea. Like as not none would mark me, but I would not chance it.'

'Why should you be remarked?' she persisted.

Reynaud drew in a sharp breath and exhaled it slowly. This, too, he remembered of her as a child;

she questioned everything. It was even more maddening now than it was then.

'Because,' he said, his voice quiet, 'it was I who killed their count.'

Her eyes widened. 'But why?'

'It was an accident. In a tournament at Ascalon, after I was knighted. His lance broke. Mine did not. This…' he patted the grey's muscular neck '…was once his horse. And the sword I carry, and my helmet…were also his.'

She stared at him, her eyes darkening to the colour of steel. Then the thick lashes dropped, hiding her feelings. She lifted her reins and stepped her mare forwards, past him. He let her take the lead, and they rode in tense silence until late afternoon, skirting golden fields and vineyards lush with purple grapes. The ripe, slightly sour smell of fermenting fruit blended with the sharp scent of hay crushed beneath their horses' hooves. The heavy, still air aggravated his unease.

He kept his gaze riveted on Leonor's stiff back. She was close to exhaustion, he knew. Still, she did not sway or slump in the saddle. She had not even asked for water these past three hours. His heart swelled in reluctant admiration.

Would to God she would prove as resolute when they reached their destination. He had no idea what awaited them in Carcassonne.

At dusk, he called a halt. When his voice rang out behind her, Leonor closed her eyes in relief. She could go no farther! Her thighs stung from the long hours in the saddle. Her bottom ached. And the suffocating heat—*ay de mi!* She could not travel another step.

She pulled her knee up and over the saddle horn and slipped off the mare. Reaching up behind the cantle, she untied her cloak and one thin woollen blanket, even though the air was so heavy she would need neither unless it rained. Neither would they need a fire. Late summer nights in Languedoc were as hot and humid as nights in Granada. And, she admitted grudgingly, more dangerous.

She wandered towards the river that purled a few yards away, then glanced back through the lacework of leafy beech trees where Reynaud was spreading a travel carpet and arranging the food packet in the centre. Then he tramped off through the thick brush to the river's edge.

Exhausted and sweaty, she slipped upstream to bathe. Just as she stepped to the river bank she glanced to her left and her heart stopped. Through a feathery screen of tamarisk she could see Reynaud. She watched him raise his arms over his head and stretch his body, rotating his shoulders and neck. Then he brought his hands to the belt at his waist and began to undo it.

The heady, scented air closed over her nose and mouth, and for a fleeting moment she could not breathe. She gulped a lungful of air, then another, as Reynaud unbuckled his sword belt and laid it aside. He pulled off his chainmail shirt and padded gambeson and dropped it where he stood. His smooth, bare skin glistened with perspiration.

'Oh!' she breathed. Instantly she clapped her hand over her mouth. He was marvellously well formed! Hard muscle ridged his upper torso, the dark hairs on his chest broken by a curving white scar. Fine dark curls peppered his abdomen.

The sight of him half-clothed made her feel hot and cold all at once. His hands, large and purposeful, began to untie his breeches.

Leonor fixed her gaze on her leather boots. *You must not watch him.* Yet she could not look away. He moved further downstream, towards a wide place in the river, loosening his breeches as he walked.

He bent to pull off his drawers, and she sucked in her breath, opening her mouth to warn him of her presence.

Nay, perhaps she should not. He was angry enough with her as it was. She would silently withdraw, move further upstream and dip her scorching face in the cooling river.

Before she could move, Reynaud stripped off the last of his garments and, keeping his back to her, moved to the water's edge. Her limbs froze. He arched his body and plunged into the blue-green pool where the current eddied, and she heard the water ripple as he swam back and forth. Ah, she wanted to peel off her tunic and trousers and curve her tingling body into the water beside his.

She expelled a long, uneven breath. She felt something extraordinary inside, a fluttering in her belly, and she knew it was because of this tall, black-haired man arching his body in the water. In spite of everything—her grief at how he had changed, her annoyance at the pace he set for travel in the sweltering heat, his short temper and gruff manner—in spite of all that, she respected him. Trusted him. She *liked* him.

In fact, she had never known a man she liked as well.

He stroked to the bank and hauled himself out of the river, water streaming over his face and chest from his unruly dark curls. Half-turning his body towards the opposite bank, he raised both arms and smoothed his hair back with his hands.

'You are beautiful.'

She had spoken aloud without realising it.

Reynaud stood stock still, his naked back to her. 'Leonor. Cousin. Do not say such things to me.'

She swallowed convulsively. 'Why not? You are my cousin, as you say. More than that, Rey, you are a Templar. You are pledged to Christ. Likely you are not interested in women.'

With a groan, Reynaud felt his body stir as he turned to her. 'I am your cousin, it is true. And a Templar. But,' he added, his voice hoarse, 'I am also a man.'

A sweet, drowsy liquor flowed like rich wine through her veins. The air between them crackled with awareness.

In the quiet glade a cicada began a faint humming, as if the earth were moaning as it turned under her feet. A hot throbbing bloomed in the place between her thighs.

An image floated into her mind of a waterwheel, rising, then plunging into a stream, seeding the barren earth with new life. Caught up in an undercurrent she only half-understood, her body responded to the rhythm of life that pulsed deep within her.

She wanted to touch him.

His eyes darkened into fathomless emerald pools. His desire for her was obvious, and he took a single step towards her.

Chapter Twelve

Leonor turned away from Reynaud, her body trembling, and he moved forwards to stand at her back. 'Look at me,' he commanded. 'Turn and look at me.'

She turned, her mouth suddenly dry. She had never before seen a naked man.

'I am a Templar, who serves God,' he said, his voice low. 'But that makes me no less a man.' He flicked his glance downwards, between his thighs. 'The body knows what it is, even if the spirit wills it otherwise.'

Her heart surged into her throat. Through the roaring in her ears she heard the distant rumble of thunder. Somewhere it was raining, bringing cooling water to the earth's parched skin. Unconsciously she ran her tongue over her lips.

But it was not raining here. Here, her breasts were swelling and her most private parts ached with desire. She yearned for him in the most carnal, sinful way!

A net dropped over her heart and drew tight. All these years she had searched for a man unlike others, had longed to be united in spirit and in body with that one man. She had waited for him all her life.

And, oh, sweet heaven, now she feared she had found him! It was *this* man she hungered for. A monk. One who, by his own choice, was pledged to God.

And chastity.

She wanted to weep, to laugh, to tear at her hair—anything to relieve the hunger of her flesh for the wrong man. A man whose inner scars threatened to crush her joy at being alive.

She shut her eyes and raised her face towards the purpling sky. *God, God help me! Surely I, your faithful servant, do not deserve this heavenly jest? What have I done that You reward me thus?*

'Leonor.' Reynaud breathed her name. 'Lea.'

Her blood raced at the sound of his voice, throaty with need. A thrush began its song, then broke off as suddenly as it had started. Her chest tightened until she could scarcely draw breath. *Sing*, she willed the bird. *Sing, so I will not have to speak.*

'Leonor.'

'Say nothing, Reynaud.'

'I must. Leonor, hear me.'

'I cannot. Will not,' she amended. Neither could she look at him. She squeezed her lids tight and clenched her hands at her sides. But underneath she knew it was no use. All at once she knew the truth. She loved him. She had always loved him.

Like a soft breath, a mist of rain dropped a veil over them. Very slowly Reynaud turned her to face him. A mere arm's length away from her trembling form, he was grateful for the cooling drops that pelted his bare skin. Only as reason returned could he risk looking into her eyes, acknowledging the longing he saw reflected in their grey depths. All his life he had wanted a woman to look at him in that way.

He dared not touch her. If she made one gesture, one small movement towards him, he would be lost.

The rain settled into a whispery rhythm. His flesh cooled, then heated anew as he watched her pupils widen and darken with passion. Her peaked nipples showed under her damp tunic.

He willed his still tumescent body into stone, prayed that she would not reach out to him and shatter his last vestige of self-control. Ecstasy— madness, even—lay just a heartbeat away.

His hands burned. He dug both thumbs into the flesh of his thighs. Lust was a rack of fire, the turning of the wheel that breaks the body into flame. He closed his eyes, ordered himself to turn his back to her.

Rain stung his shoulders. If he looked at her again, saw the tears sheening her face, sparkling on the feathery sweep of dark lashes, his heart would burst.

The moment stretched. His blood throbbed in his veins. To keep himself from touching her, he turned away.

'Reynaud.' She breathed his name.

He jerked, but did not open his eyes.

'Reynaud,' she repeated.

'Lea, step away from me. Now, while I still have my wits.'

He sensed her withdrawal. The heat that licked at him when she was near faded until there was nothing left but an odd emptiness and the soft hiss of the rain.

He opened his eyes. She had vanished. As if released from an enchantment, he jolted to life, grabbed his breeches and hurriedly drew them on. When he reached the horses he had tied to a tree, Leonor was draping the travel carpets over two low-branching oak limbs to form a shelter from the wet. Avoiding his gaze, she unrolled a third carpet and spread it underneath.

He moved to his saddlebag for a clean tunic. When he pulled it over his head, the rustle of oiled parchment told him Leonor was unwrapping the food packet.

'There is more bread and cheese here,' she announced, her voice uneven. 'And some grapes.' Still she would not look at him. 'Will you want—?'

'Yes,' Reynaud answered quickly. 'Some wine. Behind your saddle, rolled in a canvas sack.'

But even the wine could not quench the hunger burning inside him. When she unloaded her harp and propped it beside her on the carpet, his gut clenched. Idly she strummed her fingers across the strings and he groaned aloud.

She began to sing an old gypsy ballad.

In the next instant he strode to her side and pulled the instrument out of her hands. 'Play if you must,' he said, his voice raw. 'But, please, do not sing.'

She looked up with widened eyes. 'But my song is not blasphemous. It is only a gypsy ballad.'

'Just so,' he said. 'I—' His voice choked off.

'Rey, why are you so harsh with me? What is it that weighs on you? Is it what awaits you in Carcassonne?'

'Nay,' he lied. He knew not what to expect at Carcassonne save that whatever Grand Master de Blanquefort ordered, so would he undertake.

Leonor weighed on him. What was he to do with her? How could he secure her safety and carry out his Templar orders at the same time? Worse, how could he stand being near her for one more hour, inhaling the spice-sweet scent of her hair, her skin, hearing her soft, low voice speak his name? He knew he could not. Unable to answer, he stalked off towards the river.

When he returned he did not speak, and when she gestured at the food she had laid out, he found he could not eat. His body tense and aching, he lay down on the carpet, careful to put his back to her.

He must have slept, because the next thing he knew it was dark and Leonor lay curled like a kitten up beside him.

Leonor awoke to water dripping from leaves overhead to the sodden earth, making irregular soft plopping sounds. Much like her heartbeat, she thought. Beside her, Reynaud slept, his breathing deep and steady. She lay still, gazing out past the edge of the carpet tent she had fashioned.

The round golden moon hung low in the sky, like a great ripe fruit floating behind a netting of dark clouds. When it broke through, warm light poured down through the trees and she smiled into the dark. The storm had blown over.

And the storm in her heart? She lay motionless, savouring the warmth of Reynaud's body next to hers. She wanted him.

And he wanted her. She had seen it in his eyes, heard it in his voice. She drew in a lungful of the sweet-scented night air. Reynaud was the most intriguing mix of a man she had ever known. And the most lost. And the most handsome.

Such a man was wasted as a Templar.

The squire Galeran lifted Count Henri's chainmail hauberk from the battered wooden barrel at his feet. Humming to himself, he smoothed his fingers over the burnished metal and nodded in satisfaction. The tumbling sand had scrubbed off most of the rust; the rest he would polish with oil and pumice until it gleamed like silver once again.

He seated himself on the stool outside the stable door and bent to his task, singing under his breath. *'My love is like a skylark, a nightingale so fair…'* He sang the words haltingly as he worked over the metal coils with a worn linen rag and a boar-bristle brush, trying to visualise the lute accompaniment he had learned the day before. *'A woman is sweeter than honey...'* or...or was it lilies? That was it, lilies. He sighed. *'A woman is...'*

In his mind's eye, the lady Leonor materialised, seated at her harp, tossing her black hair over her shoulders. His polishing slowed, then stopped.

Leonor. Such a beautiful name, like music on the tongue. When would she return from her journey with the Templar? They were travelling north, he remembered. Perhaps to Mont-de-Marsan? Or east, towards Tarbes and Toulouse? He knew only that her journey would end at his father's castle at Carcassonne. And then, might she not tell his father the count about her faithful squire? How pleased she was by his service?

Ah, Papa would be so proud of him.

He applied himself once again to the metal garment spread over his knees. *'She is both earthly paradise and joy,'* he sang as he worked. *'And she is—'*

A shadow fell over him and he broke off.

'You are the squire Galeran?' a hard, rasping voice demanded.

Galeran leaped up, knocking over the stool in his haste. 'Yes, my lord. How may I serve you?' He clutched the heavy mail shirt in both hands and stared at the bulky knight in Hospitaller dress.

The knight dismounted and loomed over him. Suddenly his arm shot out and a hand seized the neck of Galeran's tunic. 'You may indeed serve me, boy.' He gave a vicious upwards tug. 'You know the Templar Reynaud?'

Galeran struggled to keep his balance. 'That I do, my lord.'

'Then you also know that he is no longer here in Moyanne.'

Galeran nodded, barely able to breathe.

'There's a good lad. And do you also know where he has gone?'

Galeran shook his head so hard it ached.

The knight's bushy eyebrows drew downwards. 'No? Must I then refresh your memory?' He lifted one thick hand, closing it into a huge fist under Galeran's nose.

The squire's mind raced. 'It will do no good to cuff me, lord. I am…forgetful, you see. I forget everything—names, places. I even forgot to clean my uncle's mail yestereven, and today—'

His voice choked off as the knight's fingers squeezed the neck of Galeran's tunic tight about his throat.

'This matter I think you have not forgotten,' the knight said through gritted teeth. 'You will tell me where they have gone.'

Think! Galeran reminded himself. Stall. Perhaps some help will come. *I will lie, if I must. God will forgive me.*

'They?' he wheezed. His legs shook so violently he could scarcely stand.

'You know very well who "they" are. Lady Leonor and the Templar.'

'Well,' Galeran managed, 'let me think. And you are certain that they travel together? The Lady Leonor and—'

The knight slapped the back of his free hand across Galeran's face. 'You have until I count to ten, boy.' He hit him again, palm up. 'And then…'

Galeran blanched. *And then?* The blood drained from his upper body, leaving a cold lump where his heart should be. *Oh, merciful God, help me. Or at least give me the courage to do what I must.*

'One.'

'I— Well, you see, my lord—'

'Two.'

'It's this way, my lord. The two of them—Lady Leonor, you say? And—'

'Three.'

'Reynaud, the Templar. It is Reynaud you m-mean, is it n-not?' Galeran's tongue stumbled over the words he babbled in desperation.

'Four.' The knight's eyes took on an unsettling, fixed look that turned Galeran's blood to ice.

'Five.'

Galeran's face ached. Fighting back tears, he tried to concentrate. 'Wait.'

'Six.' The voice dropped to a menacing whisper. 'Seven.'

Sweat poured down Galeran's neck. Should he call for help? Scream? Like as not if he did, the knight would throttle him then and there. Besides, no one could hear him over the shouts of men training on the jousting field. What could he do?

'Eight.'

'Very well, then, I will tell you,' Galeran lied. 'Only release me so I can catch my breath.'

'You have breath enough to beg, you brat. Use it to tell me where they have gone.'

'My lord, I—'

'Nine.'

Galeran closed his eyes. He would not betray them, no matter what came. He could not, for Leonor's sake. *Ah, would that he did not love her and could save himself. How he wanted to live.*

A violent jerk on his tunic pulled him off balance, and the next thing he knew he was being dragged into a cool, musty smelling place. The stables.

Oh, no. No. He didn't want it to be in the stables. Not the stables.

'Ten.'

Chapter Thirteen

Reynaud awoke to see the moon riding high against a curtain of black velvet. Through the opening in the tent of carpets Leonor had fashioned, he watched wisps of cloud drift in lacy patterns across the silvery globe. He had seen moonglow such as this in Syria, but on the battlefield. Then he had cringed from the light because it revealed to the ever-vigilant Saracens the number of Templar knights and their position.

Now, he welcomed the pale glow. At his leisure, he could watch Leonor's face as she slept beside him. He raised himself on one elbow. Never would he have enough of looking at her. And lying next to her…it made his senses swim.

With a murmur, Leonor rolled to one side, away from him. Reynaud curved his body around hers, laying his arm across her waist and pulling her spine tight against his chest. Bending his legs, he cupped her bottom between his knees and his groin.

She moaned in her sleep and snuggled into him, like a kitten seeking warmth. The movement was so enticing he groaned aloud. Here, nestled together in the quiet tent, holding Leonor in his arms, was the closest he would ever come to heaven on this earth. Part of him wished never to arrive at Carcassonne.

But another part—the knight with obligations to his Grand Master—would rise when dawn broke and ride on to his destination, as he had been ordered.

He did not want to think about what awaited him in Carcassone at this moment. He knew he would have to leave her, and then… A bruised feeling filled his chest.

At first light, he rose quietly, pulled on his boots and made his way over the rain-dampened ground to the river. By the time Leonor poked her head out of the tent, he had his destrier and her cream mare saddled and ready.

'We leave at once, I see.' Her low voice showed no surprise, only resignation. Her eyes met his. 'I had thought to break our fast.'

'No,' Reynaud said, more sharply than he intended.

'No,' she echoed. 'It is always no.' She scrambled out of the tent and stood before him, her eyes flashing. 'You are still angry with me, that I know. But I am hungry!'

'We will eat as we ride. Come.' He stepped forwards. He heard her quick intake of breath and closed his eyes. *How hard it was to keep from touching her, as he longed to…as a man touched a woman.*

He had to remind himself he was not his own man, but God's. 'I will pack up the shelter,' he said, working to keep his voice light. 'Go and wash.'

She nodded shortly and spun away. He watched her stomp a careless path through the damp undergrowth. She had spirit, that one. And her mind was quick as a fox's. Something told him they would need both in the days to come.

The stark stone walls of Carcassonne loomed on the hill above her. Leonor tipped her head back and scanned the length of the fortress battlements in amazement. Truly, she had never seen the like.

The structure covered the entire hilltop overlooking the red-tiled roofs of the village and the River Aude below. On the north-west corner, a square watch tower jutted into the cerulean sky. Rounded towers with arrow slits interrupted the rambling expanse of smooth, weathered grey stone. Turrets bristled along the ramparts.

They moved closer. Outside the walls, workmen were digging into the dark earth, settling posts that outlined a grassy area just below the largest of the moss-covered towers. At their approach, one of the men, a burly fellow with tanned forearms and a weathered face, straightened and doffed his worn felt cap.

'Come to join the lists, have ye?' He gestured at the imposing castle behind him. 'Draws 'em like flies to honey, she does,' he continued amiably. '*La pucelle du Languedoc,* that's what Lord Roger calls 'er. Though that castle's a bit old to be a "maiden", eh?'

Without waiting for an answer, he bent again over the post he was positioning.

They urged their mounts up the steep slope towards the arched stone gateway. 'Remember the squire, Galeran?' Leonor asked. 'The one who helped us in Moyanne?'

'Aye,' Reynaud said. 'What of him?'

'He is Count Roger's son. Roger is Uncle Henri's younger brother.'

Reynaud merely grunted. Leonor flashed a quick look at him. 'You are not listening. You are thinking of the lists, are you not?'

When he did not answer, she sighed. 'How like a man. You simply cannot resist the challenge of a tournament. Will you enter?'

'I have had enough of fighting. Even in tourneys. There are always younger knights eager to prove their mettle. The herald's roster will spill over with names. Besides—'

'Besides,' she interjected, 'you have some mission or other for your Grand Master.'

'Aye.'

Her heart squeezed. She could not help but wonder about his mission. Her pulse suddenly pounding, she turned her mare away and lifted her face towards the hilltop fortress. Side by side, they moved forwards, towards the castle gate.

Abruptly Reynaud pulled up on his reins, then leaned down, caught her mare's bridle and tugged her horse to a halt beside his. Leaning towards her, he spoke in a low voice.

'Leonor, I would say something to you before we enter this place.'

She looked up at him and blanched at what she saw. Heat burned in the usually cool green eyes. All at once it was if she could see into his soul. He feared something.

'I know not what awaits me here,' he said.

She clenched her hands on the reins. 'Will you be in danger?'

He looked away, his jaw tight, and did not answer.

'Rey?'

An awareness bloomed between them, an intangible bond that had always been there, now honed to agonising clarity like the taut wire of a rope dancer.

'I would have you safe,' he said at last.

'I will be safe. Count Roger commands many strong knights.' She licked her dry lips. 'But I do not want to reach the castle, only to have you leave me.'

He nodded without speaking.

'Oh, Rey, I wish we could stay here for ever outside the walls. Outside of time and the demands of duty.'

'You know we cannot,' he said hoarsely.

'Yes,' she said on a sigh. 'That I know well.'

He caught her arm. 'If there is aught else of spying in your plans, you must forgo it.'

'I…I do not intend to spy. I want to come with you on your mission!'

'No.'

'Rey—?'

'No.'

Her shoulders drooped and she turned away. 'Then I have no choice but to play my harp and sing here at this castle. It is what I have always wanted, and yet…'

'As a woman, you should want other things.'

She licked her dry lips. 'Will you think of me? As I will you?'

'Aye,' he said shortly. He pulled her closer. 'You are never far from my thoughts.'

'We have reached the gate, Rey. We must go forwards, or…'

Without speaking he released her and prodded his mount into motion. Their horses clacked over the cobblestone paving like iron nails jangling against chainmail.

She followed Reynaud through the gatehouse and into the outer bailey. Looming stone towers threw long shadows over the huge square keep and various outbuildings, servants' huts and a small, gracefully rounded structure she took to be the chapel. The cobbled paving stretched past the armoury to a long building with a red-tile roof. The bakehouse, she guessed, from the yeasty smell of bread drifting on the late afternoon air. An officious-looking woman in a flour-splotched apron was shoving a flat wooden paddle laden with rounded loaves of bread into the oven.

Her stomach rumbled. If many knights were expected for the tournament, this evening's meal should be festive, and the dishes served plentiful.

They skirted the pantry shed where four plucked pheasants hung, neck down, and her mouth watered.

Reynaud's destrier startled a dozen black-and-white chickens into a squawking phalanx, but he did not alter his pace. Without swerving, he headed for the entrance to the main keep. Through another stone gatehouse, then the wooden drawbridge creaked down to admit them.

The iron portcullis hung poised over her head, its sharpened points bared like so many metal teeth. She shivered until she reached the safety of the inner ward where servants took her reins and helped her dismount. She untied her harp and reluctantly handed it to a page not much taller than the instrument itself.

Reynaud slung his heavy saddlebags over one shoulder, and their horses were led away to be fed and groomed. The young page stumbled under the harp's weight, and Reynaud lifted the instrument into his own hands. Leonor exhaled a sigh of relief. Being separated from her instrument always made her uneasy.

'Inform Lord Roger he has guests from Moyanne,' Reynaud ordered the page.

The boy raced off and her eyes locked with Reynaud's. Now they would separate, she to bathe and see to her garments before the evening meal, and he to…whatever it was that men did before supper. No doubt she would be given a private chamber, but Reynaud might end up in the knights' barracks, or worse, sleeping on the floor of the main hall, rolled up in his cloak.

Did he know the layout of this castle? Would he know where she would sleep? Which passageway, which staircase?

Something niggled in her brain, something that had haunted her ever since they had ridden away from Moyanne. Bernard de Rodez. By now the Hospitaller must know of their true destination.

She would never forget that odd, feral light in the knight's milky eyes when he had closed his fingers over her wrist and squeezed. He had hurt her. He had intended to hurt her.

A finger of ice slid up her spine. What would he do to her if he found her again?

'I bid you welcome, Sir Templar,' a hearty voice boomed. 'And your…lady, too, if this youth beside you is what I surmise.'

A towering beanpole of a man dressed in an elegant cream-silk tunic studied Leonor with a practised eye. 'Clever of you to travel thus disguised, my lady. And a harper, too? Just in time, both of you. Welcome. Welcome!'

Count Roger bowed to Leonor and clasped one arm around Reynaud's shoulders. Reynaud offered a courteous salute. 'I am called Reynaud, my lord. Lately from the Holy Land.'

The count made a half-turn towards him, studying him with friendly eyes. He had long, dark hair, a thick beard and eyes like his brother Henri, blue as summer's sky.

'With me,' Reynaud continued, 'is my cousin, Leonor de Balenguer y Hassam, of Granada. I bring greetings from your brother, Count Henri, in Moyanne.'

'Aha, from Henri? That is fine, fine indeed!' the resonant voice bellowed. 'A pity he could not attend the tourney himself and bring my son, Galeran, with him. But— Jannet?' he called over his shoulder. 'Jannet! Come, greet our guests. *Jannet!*'

At a rustle on the staircase, Leonor turned to see a round-faced young woman glide to her husband's side.

'You are most welcome,' she trilled. Her voice held a hint of laughter, and beneath her crisp white linen headdress sparkled a pair of merry black eyes. 'From Moyanne, you say?' She slanted the count a dimpled smile. 'How fares my stepson, Galeran?'

'He is well, my lady,' Leonor responded. 'And a fine lad. Indeed, he was most helpful at our departure.'

'Oh, do please call me Jannet. And I may call you…?'

She turned an expectant face on Leonor.

Leonor smiled in response to the young woman's infectious good spirits, 'I am called Leonor.'

'Leonor! A lovely name.' She clasped Leonor's hands in her own. 'Why, we are almost sisters in age, are we not? I am but twenty and four, too young for my Lord Roger, some say, who is more than twice that many summers.'

Jannet flashed another dazzling smile in her husband's direction. 'But he does not mind, do you, sweet? 'Tis May and December between us, but in our hearts, 'tis sweetest summer.'

Her laughter bubbled forth and she linked her husband's arm with her own. Leonor watched a blush darken the count's cheeks. He opened his mouth to speak, then closed it and shrugged.

'Oh,' Jannet chimed, 'I have said too much again, have I not?' She stood on tiptoe to brush her lips against the count's chin. 'I will hear of this at bedtime, no doubt,' she murmured to Leonor with a giggle.

Leonor fought back laughter. Jannet tugged her husband's arm around her waist and addressed Reynaud. 'Do you enter the tourney the day after tomorrow?'

'Nay, lady, that I do not. I do not stay for the tourney. I must ride on.'

'Oh?' The count's dark eyebrows rose. 'Where do you travel, then, if not to the famous lists of *la pucelle du Languedoc*?'

Reynaud hesitated. The truth was, he had not an inkling. Someone in Carcassonne—an agent for de Blanquefort—was to instruct him upon his arrival. His new orders would take him somewhere to the south, he guessed. The exact location of Templar head-quarters in southern France was a well-kept secret.

'Come, Sir Reynaud,' the count boomed in his ear. 'Let us see how the field being prepared for the lists is coming. I've a dozen workmen setting the posts at this very hour.'

Purposefully, the count disengaged himself from his wife and, giving her a surreptitious pat on the bottom, drew Reynaud towards the door. 'You can bathe and refresh yourself later, there is plenty of time.'

Reynaud handed the harp to a man at arms lounging against a wall and followed the count.

Their masculine voices faded, and Leonor found herself alone with Jannet. The young woman scanned her rumpled trousers and travel-stained tunic.

'Do join me in my chamber, Leonor. We must find you something to wear for the feast tonight. Something elegant. Something…startling. Ah! I have just the gown in my chest. I cannot wait until you try it on!'

Leonor laughed in spite of herself. Jannet's high spirits were contagious, and she certainly needed cheering. The count's young wife was just what she needed tonight—the last night before Reynaud departed.

'Come!' Jannet sang. 'Your chamber will be next to mine, on the top floor. Oh, do let us hurry!' She signalled the sturdy man at arms to follow with Leonor's harp.

The stocky man groaned good-naturedly and followed the two women up the three narrow stone staircases. At the threshold of the airy chamber Jannet indicated she was to occupy, Leonor paused.

Sunshine flooded in through the narrow leaded-glass window, pouring golden light on the tapestries hung to soften the stone walls. A small bed, the green damask curtains cleverly sewn to form a canopy, stood against one wall, flanked by two small tables of dark wood.

The man at arms settled the harp in one corner and with a nod left the two women alone.

'Your…companion, Reynaud, is very handsome,' Jannet remarked with a grin. 'He looks deliciously uncombed—his hair, I mean. 'Tis so black and fine, and curls this way and that like an unruly boy's. And what eyes! Like spring grass or… I know! They are the exact colour of summer sage.'

'I am not familiar with that herb,' Leonor ventured in an attempt to change the subject.

'Ah, in Bretagne, where my home was, there were fields and fields of it growing wild.' She flashed a teasing glance at her. 'Like your Reynaud, in a way. And in winter,' she added quickly, taking Leonor's hand in her own, 'the colour darkens. That,' she murmured with a smile, 'is how the knight Reynaud looks at you, like winter and summer blended. Have you not noticed?'

Her cheeks grew hot. 'I—' She did not want to lie to Jannet. The young woman's candour invited honesty, not evasion. 'I have noticed, yes.'

Jannet laughed. 'For a moment I was afraid you might be simple.'

Leonor laughed. 'That I am not.'

'Good! I am starved for talk, and a companion who is simple would truly be worse than talking with the old women and servants when a tiresome crusade takes away all the men.' Jannet dimpled and gave her a quick hug. 'Oh, Leonor, I am so very glad you have come!'

Leonor impulsively returned the hug. Jannet's good will and girlish prattle would dull the pain of Reynaud's leaving.

Then her laughter drained away and suddenly she could not draw breath. Oh, what if she never saw on him again?

Chapter Fourteen

The door banged open, and two brawny servants rolled a huge oak tub into Reynaud's chamber. Behind them trooped a cadre of attendants, each armed with a bucket of steaming water. They filled the tub until the water sloshed over the sides, left a pile of fresh towels, a dish of yellow soap and a jar of herbs within reach, and then withdrew.

He sniffed the fragrant soap—lavender and roses. Did all the knights of Languedoc smell this sweet? Shucking off his travel-stained garments, he lay back in the steaming tub and let his eyelids drift shut. He was tired and sweaty, and his old thigh wound throbbed, but at least Leonor was safe in Carcassonne.

He pictured Count Roger being bathed by his young wife in the privacy of their chamber and could not suppress the chuckle that slipped out. Count Roger no doubt bathed *with* his wife. A lusty man, that. He had seen the gleam in the count's eye when he looked on his lady. Desire for her was writ all over him.

His lids snapped open. He should not chastise the man for such feelings. Was he not wrestling with his own desire for a woman?

He grasped the dish of soap, dipped his fingers in and smoothed the perfumed paste over his chest and belly. He would emerge from his tub perfumed like a violet.

At least he would smell like nobility.

But nobility he was not. He had not been born to lands or titles, as Count Roger had. Reynaud's breeding was only skin deep. He had learned his manners from Hassam and from Hugh de Montfort, the knight who had trained him as his squire.

He breathed in the warm, jasmine-scented evening air wafting from the open casement and his thoughts drifted to Leonor, the cool grey eyes that heated under his gaze, the light, sweet smell of her skin. His groin began to ache.

In Leonor's presence he was once again beginning to feel glad he was alive. Parting from her would tear him in two.

His throat tightened into a knot. He was beginning to understand what drove a man into the arms of a woman. It was not the body's hunger, but the drive of the spirit for oneness.

Clasping a clean linen towel around his waist, he stepped out of the wooden tub and dried himself so vigorously his skin tingled, then stopped abruptly as a disturbing thought surfaced. With Count Roger's tournament planned, knights both honourable and wayward would be everywhere. They could not help but notice Leonor, seek her company. Perhaps even accost her.

He clenched his jaw, drew on the fresh tunic laid out on the canopied bed, then dropped the white Templar surcoat over his head. In the fading light, the crimson cross was dark as blood. The garment reminded him he was bound to God. Such a calling was not something a man could offer a woman.

A light tap sounded on the door. Reynaud jammed on his leather boots, strode forwards favouring his right leg, and jerked the door open.

A young boy cowered before him, his face white against the forest-green tunic worn by Count Roger's pages.

'M-my lord, you are w-wanted below.'

Reynaud bent down stiffly on one knee, lowered himself to eye level with the boy and gentled his voice. 'Who is it that sends thee, lad?'

'A m-man, my lord. He did not give his name, but sent me straight away to fetch you.' The page clenched and unclenched his small hands. 'He s-said to come to the postern gate, behind the stables. Something 'bout a silver swan.'

At last. His orders were to be delivered to him. Reynaud rose carefully and lifted his sword belt from the chest. For some reason his hands trembled.

'Show me,' he commanded, buckling the length of leather about his hips. While the page watched, wide-eyed, he thrust his sword into the leather scabbard, then slid a slim curved dagger between his surcoat and the sword belt. Already his belly was knotted like a braid of onions.

The boy pivoted and pointed down a narrow, darkened staircase. 'That way.'

Before he could take a step, the page darted ahead. 'Follow me, my lord. I know the way.'

The staircase led to a doorway, little used from the look of the rusty hinges, then on through to the outside wall of the keep. With wary eyes, he skirted the castle, staying close to the curtain wall as he followed the boy towards the stables.

The page pointed again. 'Behind there, my lord. You go first, will you, my lord? He—he frightens me.'

'You need go no further, lad.' Reynaud pressed a coin into the small, sticky hand. 'My thanks for your service.'

The page darted away into the dusky shadows, and Reynaud stared after the small form. It seemed only yesterday he himself was that age, eager for adventure, heedless of the cost. Now, he was weary in spirit and aching from old wounds. *How short life was.*

He inhaled the musty scent of horse dung and hay and stepped into the deepening gloom between the stable and the curtain wall and found himself facing an alcove built into the stone. Pale light winked from an arrow slit at its centre.

A voice spoke from the shadowed embrasure. 'Reynaud?'

He jerked towards the sound. 'I am Reynaud. Who is it that calls?'

'A friend.'

He peered into the enclosure, tightening his hand on his sword hilt. 'Show yourself, then.'

A whisper of cloth, then a shrouded figure unfolded itself from the shadows, looked carefully to left and right and straightened before Reynaud. Gold-flecked brown eyes stared into his.

'Your name?' Reynaud demanded.

'Brother...Pierre.'

'From?'

'Saint-Foy de Conques,' came the quick answer.

Reynaud studied the narrow, lined face before him and held out one arm. 'Greetings to you, then, Brother Pierre. Your business?'

Brother Pierre grasped his hand in the secret Templar handshake, thin lips twitching. '*Your* business it is, I fear.'

Reynaud raised his eyebrows and waited in silence. The brown-robed monk hesitated, coughed and hesitated again. 'I suppose I must tell you sooner or later. It is just that—'

Reynaud's gut clenched. 'Tell me, then, and be done with it.'

'It will not be easy, my son.' Brother Pierre lowered his voice. 'Granted, Bertrand de Blanquefort has great faith in your prowess in the field, as well as your skill in...diplomacy, shall we say? But there is a limit to what one man—even one such as yourself—can do.'

Reynaud's heart began to pound. The man paused, tapping one lean forefinger against his lined cheek. 'Still, de Blanquefort must have his reasons, so here it is.'

The monk bent his legs at the knees and sank downwards until his angular frame rested on his haunches. The shapeless brown habit settled on the ground about him like the shroud of a nesting guinea hen.

The monk poked a bony finger at the hard-packed earth and drew a crude map. 'Here sits a chateau. A small fortress, let us say. A resting place for—' he shot a glance at Reynaud, kneeling beside him '—a treasury of gold.'

Reynaud nodded, careful to keep his expression blank. 'And?'

With his fingernail the monk scratched a mark on to the earth. 'And here is the only gate to this fortress. It is heavily guarded. Now do you see?'

Reynaud drew in a careful breath. 'I see that whatever treasure lies within those walls is sought after by others, and that whoever controls the gate, controls the treasure. Louis of France, most likely.'

'Exactly. But what lies inside does not belong to Louis. In fact, Louis knows nothing of its existence. It is the treasury of the Knights Templars. By God's law, it belongs to the Pope.'

Reynaud narrowed his eyes. 'The king of France sets himself against the Holy Father?'

Brother Pierre nodded and dropped his voice to a murmur. 'De Blanquefort is the pope's man, but the fortress, Rennes-le-Château, now belongs to Louis. It came to him from a vassal who died without issue.'

'Why not simply attack and drive off the French king's knights?'

The monk laid his frail hand on Reynaud's arm. 'No, my boy. You see, it works two ways. Louis does not know of the secret hiding place inside the walls. And the Pope—' Brother Pierre grinned and shrugged his shoulders '—thinks to keep the treasure safe. So, why not let Louis of France protect it for him?'

Reynaud rose to his feet. 'Why tell me of this?'

The monk squinted up at him in the dim light. 'Because, my son, the only way to add gold to the treasury is to infiltrate the château. Your orders are to slip past Louis's forces at the château gate and deposit the gold you carry for the Templars inside the château. In this way, the treasure increases, you see.' He smiled, but it did not reach his eyes. 'Louis does not know of the treasury. Nor does he suspect that under his royal nose, the Pope's golden goose grows fat.'

Reynaud snorted. 'Slip past…? And live to tell of it?'

'Mayhap not,' Brother Pierre replied, his voice calm. 'But perhaps, if it be the will of God.'

Reynaud's stomach somersaulted. 'One man against an entire fortress? It is a fool's errand.'

The monk drew himself up to Reynaud's level and reached a claw-like hand towards the scarlet cross sewn on his surcoat. 'That it is not, Reynaud. It is an order from your Grand Master.'

His heart thumped to a stop. So this was his mission, to bring the gold the Pope needed to hire mercenaries to fight Louis of France. He spat on to the dirt. The perfidy of Christian against Christian disgusted him. Was he to risk his life for a rivalry between pope and king? Likely he would die obeying such an order.

A sick feeling flooded his belly. He had sworn to obey his Grand Master, and the vows of a Templar were broken only at the price of an ignominious death. He had no choice.

The distant sound of pipe and tabor, laughter and raucous voices floated on the air. Somewhere life was not in jeopardy, it was simply being lived. He thought of the years before he had taken his vows, the years when he had felt free. Then he had questioned everything.

Now he obeyed orders.

Suddenly he wondered at himself, questioning such orders. Was he turning into a rebel? One part of him wanted to fulfil his obligation; another part wanted…wanted…? An unsettling chill crawled up his backbone. There were no words to describe the hunger he felt.

He felt that he *was* two people. *Another person lived inside his body, one he never knew existed.*

He must obey his Grand Master. Better to die in honour than in disgrace. At least then the struggle of life in this world would hold some meaning. It was honour among men that held civilisation together.

Brother Pierre gripped Reynaud's shoulder.

'There is a secret passage, through the château curtain wall.'

A secret passage would not save him. To get to the passage he would have to breach the guarded wall itself. Alone. Death would hound his every step.

'Show me.'

Brother Pierre knelt on the ground once more. Hunching his shoulders, he scratched a few lines in the dirt, then hastily scuffed them away with his sleeve.

But not before Reynaud glimpsed the layout and shook his head in disbelief. After a long moment he stood slowly. Deliberately he tipped his face up towards the last flaming rays of the sun as it sank into evening.

How beautiful the world was. Cruel and ignorant, yes, but God in His wisdom had made it lovely for man to look upon. After half a lifetime of fighting, of treachery and death, he was finally beginning to see the beauty of the universe and let it ease his spirit.

He thought of Leonor. She was the touchstone for the joy he felt in being alive.

Tomorrow he would risk losing all he was beginning to care about. He twisted to face the monk.

'I will ride at dawn.'

Chapter Fifteen

Reynaud sipped his unwatered wine and stared unseeing at the faces along the trestle table, mulling over Brother Pierre's parting. The monk had signed the cross against his chest, looked furtively about, then slipped away into the night.

He shook his head and took a gulp of wine. He must think, must plan this trip with care. Suddenly he wanted to see Leonor, speak with her before morning. Before he rode away.

A murmur of voices rose around him, then fell into a hush. Beside him, Count Roger sucked in his breath. 'What a beauty!'

Leonor stood at the far end of the hall, her long ivory gown shimmering in the candlelight. The silk shaped itself to her body and fell into gentle folds at her feet. When she moved, the fabric glimmered as the light caught silvery threads woven into the material. A wide band of pearl-encrusted crimson silk gleamed from neckline to hem, and a narrower girdle embroidered in silver and crimson belted the gown at the waist, dipping to a vee at her belly.

She was so radiant he could not breathe.

She started towards him. When her eyes met his, a fierce drive for possession burned in his soul. He could die tomorrow, but tonight the sweet rhythm of life pulsed through him. The thrust of carnal desire bit into his groin.

He stood to greet her. Ah, how he longed to say all the gentle sweet words he could not allow himself to utter aloud. This was agony. Another hour and he would crack wide open with the need to speak. The need to lay her sweet body under his.

Her gaze caught and held his. 'Walk with me.'

Without a word he took her hand. They threaded their way through dozing hounds and bustling servants until he felt a wash of cool air on his skin. He tugged her to a stop.

'Lea, I leave tomorrow. At dawn.'

Without answering, Leonor began to climb the spiral stone staircase to the castle roof. At the rampart, she stopped and raised her face to the night sky. The scent of jasmine mixed with new-mown hay intoxicated like the rarest perfume from the East.

'Look,' she whispered.

Stars glittered like millions of tiny diamonds against the purple-black sky. 'I want to hold them,' Leonor murmured. She stretched up one hand as if to touch them, then closed her fingers into a fist and pressed it against her mouth. The ache in her breast was sharp as a honed blade. She breathed in, struggling not to weep.

'Leonor, I—' He broke off. 'I can offer you nothing. I must not even touch you as a man would.' His voice shook.

She suppressed a wild urge to laugh and turned away.

'And there is another thing,' he said, his voice quiet.

A shard of cold, hard steel lodged in her belly. She waited, listening to his uneven breath rasp in and out, her heart constricting into a tight knot. 'Say it, then.'

He moved closer and gently cupped her shoulders in his warm hands. The heat of his body seared her skin, turned her backbone to jelly. Below her belly a sweet, hot ache bloomed. The tongue of that sweetness tormented her flesh, licked at her control. Reynaud took her hands in his own, bent his head and brought them to his lips. Softly he pressed his mouth into each palm. 'Though I must leave you, know this: I am yours to command until the end of my days.'

Her control snapped. 'That,' she said, her voice choked, 'is not all that I would wish for.' She closed her eyes, biting the inside of her lower lip. She could not bear the agony of watching him ride away from her a second time in this life. This time, he might never return.

He pulled her to face him. 'Leonor.' His tone was rough as sifting gravel. 'Lea.'

She shuddered at the desperation in his voice, the

longing and pain battling in his eyes. She did not want to hear his private words of farewell. She did not want to hear a farewell at all.

She opened her mouth, but he cut her off with a tired gesture. 'Do not say you do not wish to hear me. I must speak, and it must be now.'

'I— That I know.'

'You do not know,' he returned. 'I am pledged to the death in this matter for the Templars. I gave my word on it. Should it come to that, I would die willingly, save for one thing.'

Her throat constricted so she could scarcely push words past her lips. 'And that is?'

He caught her gaze and held it. 'I would have something of you.'

'And that is?' she repeated. Her pulse began to skitter.

A muscle in his jaw twitched. 'One kiss. Tomorrow, before I depart.'

Her heart leaped. 'Yes,' she said when she could speak.

'And if I do not die, but return whole…'

She waited, unable to force air into her aching throat. Her task for Emir Yusef was completed. Now she had an even greater one facing her—waiting for Reynaud's return.

He closed his eyes. 'One night.'

She sucked in air, then looked him full in the face. 'What of your vows, Rey?'

'My vows bind me to God,' he murmured. 'But what I feel is between you and me, Lea.'

'Then,' she answered, her voice unsteady, 'it shall be as you wish.'

'It is not as I wish,' he said through gritted teeth. 'It is as it must be for me to go on living.'

'And I also, Rey.' She reached out one hand and laid it gently over his clenched fist. 'Surely you know that by now.'

He turned her hand, interlaced her fingers with his. 'Aye. May God forgive me, I do know.'

'May God forgive us both,' Leonor said quietly. 'For He alone knows both our hearts and the future.'

The sun had scarcely risen, casting a faint peach-grey light into the tiny chamber, when Leonor heard a soft tap at her door. She raised herself on one elbow, smoothed her hair back from her face as the door swung open on silent hinges.

'Reynaud,' she breathed.

He loomed in the doorway for an instant, a tall figure silhouetted in the pale light. Light glinted off the sleeves of his chainmail hauberk, visible under the Templar surcoat. Quietly he pulled the door shut behind him and she heard the soft, metallic chink of his body armour as he moved towards her.

'I leave within the hour,' he said, his voice quiet

'So soon? Has it come already, when you are to abandon me once more?' A lancet of pain stabbed her heart. 'Men lead such separate, incomprehensible lives.' She pushed down the hot lump of pain that choked her. 'Selfish lives.'

She tossed back the linen coverlet and stood up

beside the bed. The cool morning air washed her bare arms and neck. Shivering, she wrapped the silk sleeping robe Jannet had given her tight about her body and moved to the window.

'Go, then.'

'Aye, I must. But in good time.' He moved to stand behind her, so close she could feel his warm breath on the back of her neck.

'I do not want—' she began. Her voice sounded tight.

Reynaud groaned. 'That I know. You need not remind me of the effort it takes to ride away from you a second time. The first time you were but a child, and I a heedless youth who prized everything I did not yet have, but knew the value of nothing. Now…'

'Now,' she finished for him, her voice husky with unshed tears, 'is no different. My heart was broken long ago. I thought never again to feel such pain.'

'Lea,' he whispered. He placed his palms on her shoulders, tightened his fingers to grip her hard. 'Do not torment me. It is torture enough.'

She bit her lip to keep from crying out. Drawing an uneven breath, she leaned her head back until she felt his chin graze her hair. She closed her eyes, fighting for control. *I cannot keep him near me. Neither can I bear to see him go.*

He pulled her back hard against his chest and bent his head. 'After I am gone,' he murmured against the shell of her ear, 'you must take up your harp and play.'

'I cannot.'

'You can,' he said softly. 'You must. If God wills that I am to die, I would hear your music in my ear.'

Leonor shook her head. For a moment his chin lifted away from her, then he slid one arm across her waist and turned her to face him.

Try as she would, she could not stop the sobs that rose from her chest. She clung to him, her forehead buried against his neck, pressing her fingers into the metal-ringed sleeves of his hauberk until her nails ached.

'I hate you,' she sobbed, her voice muffled against his surcoat. Even with her eyes closed, she sensed his slow smile.

'God be praised,' he said carefully. 'For if you loved me, I do not know if I could stand it.'

She raised her head. His lips curved into a lopsided smile, but his darkened eyes shone with tears.

'Why could you not just kiss me and be gone? Why must you wrench my heart so with your farewell?' she sobbed.

Because he may die, a voice reminded. *Because he knows he may never see you again.*

She unclenched her fingers and moved her hands up to clasp him about the neck. 'Forgive me, Rey,' she whispered. She managed a shaky smile. 'God must indeed have forsaken you,' she jested, 'for I do love you. I have always loved you. And well you know it.'

He made no reply, but tightened his arms about her. 'Aye,' he breathed. 'God help us both.'

Slowly his hands moved up her ribcage to her shoulders, then to her face. He placed his palms on her cheeks and tipped her chin up. When his breathing steadied, he bent his head and brushed her lips with his.

Leonor's heart stopped. 'God,' she said when she could speak, 'is not going to help us.' She opened her eyes, raised her face to his. 'He is leaving it to us.'

Reynaud inhaled slowly. A flame kindled in the emerald depths of his eyes.

'So be it.' Very slowly he cupped her face with his hands and again lowered his mouth to hers. At the touch of her lips, he made a soft noise in his throat and gathered her close.

His mouth, sweet as honeyed wine, moved over hers, caressing, questioning. The taste of him was rich and dark as black plums. A hot clenching began below her belly.

At last he lifted his head and with an inarticulate sound pressed her tight against him. Dizzy, she grasped his surcoat, crushing the crimson cross in her fingers.

He reached up, unclasped her hands and set her apart from him. His mouth was not smiling now. His fine lips were hardened into a thin line.

Enclosing her hands in his, he brought them down to waist level, then pulled them behind her back until the tips of her breasts strained against him. Once more she felt his slow mouth on hers, relished his body's lingering seal on her lips. His entire frame trembled, and then she felt him straighten and release her.

'Fare you well,' he murmured. Without looking back he strode to the oak door and pulled it open.

The chamber door swung shut. She stood without moving, listening to his footsteps recede down the passageway. The faint metallic ching of his spurs echoed off the stone walls. Her heart hammering against her ribs, she ran to the narrow window and looked out.

After a long minute Reynaud's figure emerged from a shadowed doorway below and strode through the quiet bailey. A single groom waited, clutching the grey destrier's bit in both hands. Reynaud moved to the horse's side, caught up the reins and stepped into the stirrup. Swinging his leg over the animal's rump, he settled his body into the high-backed saddle and turned the stallion towards the drawbridge.

Leonor pressed her fingers hard against her mouth. Pain swirled into her chest, crushing the breath out of her. No! She could not bear it.

He stepped the warhorse to the gatehouse, and her resolve broke. Choking back a cry, she plunged through the doorway and sped down the passage, down the narrow stone staircase and into the court-yard. The hard stone paving chilled her bare feet.

'Reynaud!'

He jerked at the sound of her voice, pulled back on the reins, then sat motionless.

'Reynaud, wait!' She reached the destrier, raised her arms to the man in the saddle. He bent towards her, caught his free arm about her waist and lifted her off her feet. With a groan, he settled her on his lap.

She pulled his head down to hers. 'Come back to me,' she whispered against his lips.

'If I could strike a bargain with God,' he said, lifting his mouth from hers, 'I would offer my soul to live and return to you.'

He cut off her reply with his lips. 'As it is, Lea…' He buried his face in her loose-flowing hair, his voice suddenly hoarse. 'If I do not ride away from you this instant, I will have no soul left to bargain with.'

She knew he meant her to smile at his jest. She tried, but the corners of her mouth trembled uncontrollably. Without looking at her, he looped his finger under the silk ribbon tying the chemise at her neck and with a sharp tug tore it off and tucked it inside his surcoat. Then he lowered her gently to the ground.

Her legs would no longer support her. Only by staring down on the hard, cold stones beneath her feet was she able to keep her balance. Holding her body rigid, knees locked, fists clenched at her side, she looked up at him and managed to smile.

He raised one hand to his heart, then his lips, and finally his forehead in the traditional Arab gesture of respect. *'Ila liqa.'*

He turned the destrier away and walked it slowly across the plank drawbridge. Leonor watched him until he disappeared into the rose-shadowed dawn. *'Ila liqa,'* she breathed. *Until we meet again.*

She prayed to God they *would* meet again.

Gathering the sleeping robe about her shaking body, she turned back towards the safety of the keep.

Ma'a salaama, my Reynaud. Go in peace.

Chapter Sixteen

Benjamin folded his writing pad in half, double-wrapped it in a square of oiled vellum, and stuffed it into the bulging leather travel satchel that lay open on his desk. Even at his advanced age, with stiff joints and an aching back and legs so spindly he wondered how they carried him, his brain still worked better than most.

And he was grateful for that! Else his life would be useless as a worn-out pot.

He was not too old to travel. Galeran had not been seen about the castle grounds for two days. Rumour had it the lad had run away. Was not his home in Carcassonne? Galeran was the only son of Count Roger of Carcassonne, who had sent the boy to Moyanne for fostering with his brother, Count Henri.

The lad would head for his home. And his father.

Benjamin bent his head to buckle the flap on the leather case. 'My instinct tells me not only Galeran, but also Leonor are in Carcassonne. Ay, the spot in my heart reserved for Leonor is soft as date paste.'

With a final glance at his small chamber, he rolled his pens in a strip of sheepskin and settled them with the other items he had gathered that morning—a hard, round loaf of bread, cheese wrapped in waxed cloth, dried fish and a stained volume of Arabic poetry. Sewn into the lining of his black robe were enough gold dinars to buy a ship.

Leonor jumped at the touch of Jannet's small hand on her arm. The young woman was speaking to her, but Leonor could not make out the words over the din of laughter and the clank of plates and wine cups at the crowded trestle table. A steady stream of knights and nobles coming for the tournament had swelled the number of guests. At night, chambers were stuffed and the floor of the great hall carpeted with snoring bodies.

'Will you not enter the competition, then?' Jannet repeated.

Leonor stared at her. 'Competition? What competition?'

Jannet grinned. 'Why, the troubadour competition, of course. Have I not been telling you…?' Her laughter trilled.

'Gracious, Leonor, where do your thoughts wander? Each year when Roger holds his tourney for the knights, I arrange a competition for minstrels and troubadours. They come from far and near, in all shapes and sizes. 'Tis most interesting.'

Leonor nodded and tried to look attentive.

'It starts the day after tomorrow, after the jousting events,' Jannet went on, 'the musicians entertain in competition with each other. Heavens, one year we had the great Bernard de Ventadorn from Eleanor's court at Poitiers!'

'Oh, aye?' Leonor murmured.

Jannet eyed her with suspicion. 'Should I guess where your mind is?'

'I— In truth, Jannet, I am much distracted by the noise tonight. Forgive me.'

'Nonsense, my friend.' Jannet pressed her hand. Lowering her voice, the young woman leaned towards her. 'It is not the noise now, is it?' she coaxed, a hint of laughter in her voice.

'I notice that your handsome Templar has ridden off on some errand or other. Roger says it is none of my business, but one cannot help remarking the absence of so singular a knight, can one?'

Jannet paused, waiting. 'Can one?' she repeated, a gentle edge in her tone. She peered into Leonor's face.

'Ah, I see a blush! Come, we will withdraw to my solar, away from all this…' she waved an arm at the platter-strewn table '…where we can be private. That is, if you have eaten your fill?'

Leonor looked down at the untouched trencher heaped with cinnamon-sauced chicken and green beans boiled with leeks and mushrooms. She had not eaten a bite of it. She nodded at her hostess.

Jannet rose. 'I have some dried quince sweetmeats upstairs, hidden from Roger, who dotes on them. Let us eat some, shall we? And drink some spiced wine to wash them down. Come on!'

Leonor had to smile. Were it Reynaud who sat beside her at table, who shared even one short hour with her, she would never hide sweetmeats from him. She would feed them to him, slowly, and taste his lips after every bite.

Her face burned at the thought.

Aye, it would ease her heart to talk with Jannet, even if only about embroidery patterns and the price of Toledo needles. And a troubadour competition?

A spark of interest glowed to life. Playing her harp might help ease her anguish. Dropping a quick reverence to Count Roger, she linked arms with Jannet and the two women headed towards the staircase.

Benjamin pulled his mule to a halt at the castle gatehouse and stared up at the stone towers. 'Aye,' he puffed. 'These old bones can go not one step farther.'

He squinted to the left, one hand shading his eyes from the hot morning sunlight. Aha, tents! And a jousting field. He cast a curious eye on the double-fenced wooden enclosure, the colourful silk banners flying in the breeze.

A tournament! And a tournament meant nobles! He chortled aloud. 'Ladies!' He sighed and his voice softened. 'Perfumed scarves. Poetry.' He rolled his black eyes heavenward.

'Passion.'

Oh, foolish man. At your age likely you would joust with a drooping lance! At the thought, he drew himself up as tall as possible. He was not dead yet!

'Nonsense. At my age,' he muttered to himself, 'love's juices are just maturing, like fine aged wine.' Or…perhaps mouldy cheese? Ah well. 'Now, where in this sprawling place…' he waved one veined hand over the meadow and the walled fortress overlooking the lists '…will I find a place to lay my head tonight?'

He nudged his mule on to the plank drawbridge. He must find the mistress of the castle and beg some shelter before the tournament began. With such an event in progress, scant room would be available, even for a well-known scholar. He nosed his mule across the bridge, respectfully touching two fingers to his turban at the gatehouse guards.

An hour later, comfortably housed in a cramped but clean pantry just off the kitchen, Benjamin turned his thoughts to Leonor. The Lady Jannet assured him she would appear at the evening meal to play her harp in the competition. 'But she is nervous, so if you bring news from Moyanne, stay hidden until the morrow.'

News? He had no news, save that young Galeran had run off. No doubt the boy was here at Carcassonne with his father, Lord Roger. In his concern for Leonor, Benjamin had neglected to ask about the lad.

He munched contentedly on the bread and cheese Lady Jannet had sent, closed his eyes and prepared his mind for evening prayers.

From the balcony of the solar, Leonor and Jannet watched knights in bright tunics and chainmail, squires, men at arms, nobles in embroidered silk tunics and velvet surcoats, even clerics in simple brown robes, stream through the castle gates in a steady parade of colour and the noise of clopping horses. Count Roger paced about the inner bailey, checking on the jousting arrangements. Abruptly he clapped one hand to his forehead, called for his herald and strode off to reinspect the lists.

By the evening meal, all was in readiness for the opening ceremonies on the morrow. Seated next to Jannet at the head table, Leonor nibbled morsels of partridge and leeks in ginger sauce, watching Count Roger with mixed amusement and curiosity.

The man was everywhere, welcoming old friends and lords of neighbouring domains, greeting scarlet-cloaked bishops from Beziers and abbots from the nearby Benedictine monastery. Just now, he was thundering at a young messenger who cowered before him.

'What, man? I have not sent challenge to the knights of Toulouse in jest! They say they bring women with them? *Ladies?* What in the name of all the saints for?'

'F-for the tourney, my lord.' The boy, arrayed in the blue-and-gold colours of Toulouse, held himself as rigid as possible, trying to hide his shaking hands under the hem of his short tunic. 'As you know, my lord, m-many knights wear a lady's favour on their helms. The ladies of Toulouse wish to watch their champions w-win honour and glory for them.'

Count Roger rolled his eyes towards the ceiling. 'So, they think to win glory, do they? Against my knights? The best knights in all Languedoc?' He glanced about the trestle tables, crowded shoulder to shoulder with the cream of French knighthood.

'What say you, men?' the count boomed. 'After the first day's competition, shall not the fair ladies of Toulouse smile upon *us*, instead?'

A great shout went up in the hall. Jannet sneaked a look at Leonor and shook her head. 'Men are so like children, are they not?' she murmured.

'*C'est bien!*' Count Roger muttered. 'And do not forget,' he called after the retreating messenger, 'all knights must make known their colours to the herald by noon tomorrow. Their shields shall be displayed in the courtyard, else they will be disqualified.'

The boy pivoted, bowed hurriedly and fled before Leonor could take another bite of her supper. 'Aye, Jannet, you are right. It seems men are for ever in a froth to beat each other over the head about something or other.'

Jannet dimpled. 'Even a peaceful display of martial prowess, a *joust à pleasance,* is a serious matter conducted under the façade of pageantry.'

'Thank goodness Reynaud did not enter the lists. The knights of Toulouse would like nothing better than to avenge the death of their count, Arnaud. Reynaud killed him accidentally at a tourney in the Holy Land.'

'Even so,' Jannet whispered behind her hand, 'he could have entered in disguise. It's a shame he had to go off on his mission. No pleasure game that—I would wager 'tis a venture that could cost him his life.'

A shudder crawled up Leonor's spine, and she laid her small eating knife beside the trencher. This gaudy tournament at Carcassonne, full of prancing peacocks and pretty words, was nothing compared to the grim task Reynaud might be facing. He fought not for glory or honour, but because he was so pledged.

She caught her breath. For the past few days since Reynaud had left she hadn't stopped thinking about him. Did he even now lay wounded? Perhaps dying? Why had he not told her of his destination?

'You must not brood on it,' Jannet urged. 'Think about something else. Your harp! You must take part in the troubadour competition tomorrow night.'

Her harp sat in her chamber, tuned and ready to try the *zajal* she was putting to melody. She cared not if she won the prize. She cared only that she played well, that she could move the listeners with her songs. Besides, music lifted her spirit. Playing her harp sustained her sense of herself.

Unable to swallow another bite, she whispered an excuse to Jannet, curtsied to Count Roger, and left her place at the table. She flew out of the great hall and up the narrow, twisting staircase to her chamber on the third level. At the door, she paused to catch her breath, then lifted the latch and pushed the heavy oak panel open.

Gleaming in the firelight, her harp beckoned from its place beneath the window. She moved through the doorway and took a single step towards the instrument.

A hand closed about her wrist like a manacle of iron. 'Do not cry out, lady,' a rough voice grated, 'else it will go hard with you.'

Bernard de Rodez! The Hospitaller had found her. She stared into his unblinking ice-blue eyes and a dark fear choked off her breath. Something in his expression made her scalp prickle.

'Unhand me.' Her knees felt watery, but she managed to keep her voice steady.

'Ah, no, lady. That I will not. Rather would I break this little wrist…' he tightened his fingers until her bones ached '…for the merry chase you have led me on.'

Leonor locked her knees to keep them from buckling. Cold sweat dampened the place between her shoulder blades.

'I said unhand me. For if you do not…' she raised her chin and tried to keep her voice from shaking '…I will lay complaint upon your coat of arms for abusing a lady. You will be disqualified from the tourney.'

With a growl, de Rodez released her. 'I will kill your Templar in the lists tomorrow. After that is done, I will deal with you. There are many ways to punish you for your deceit. None of them will be pleasant.'

Leonor's spine tingled as if pierced with cold needles. *Be careful,* a voice within her cautioned. *This man is even more dangerous than he appears.* She rubbed the raw skin of her wrist where his fingers had gripped her.

'Where is the Templar?' de Rodez demanded.

At once she understood why Reynaud had told her nothing of his mission. Her ignorance would protect her.

'I do not know.'

'You lie,' he shouted.

'I do not lie,' she replied, her voice cool. 'But even if I did know his whereabouts, I would not tell you.'

De Rodez snorted. 'Soon I think you will sing a different tune. So, he is gone, is he? Where, I wonder?' he muttered to himself. 'Well, no matter. All the better for what I have in mind for you.'

Leonor blinked.

A slow smile spread across the Hospitaller's lips, baring his teeth in a humourless grin. 'Surely you did not think to escape punishment for your trick?' He shrugged his massive shoulders. Caressing the hilt of the small dagger he wore in the wide leather belt about his tunic, de Rodez rocked back on his heels and leveled emotionless eyes on her.

'I advise you to take care how you conduct yourself with me.'

She stiffened. 'It is you who should take care, *Cousin*.' She spoke the final word with emphasis, reminding him that they were related, even if only by marriage. 'Should I lodge one protest against you for dishonourable conduct, you will be placed upon the barrier tomorrow, in full view of all assembled.'

The triumphant smile faded from de Rodez's face, and Leonor realised her threat had worked. His reputation meant a great deal to him.

'That we shall see, lady.' He nodded, closing his thick lips into a tight line. 'Aye, that we shall certainly see.'

Her heart pounding, she watched the bulky knight move noiselessly to her chamber door, ease it open and glide out into the passageway on silent feet. Like a great, overfed cat, she thought. A predatory, evil cat.

Her flesh crawled.

Chapter Seventeen

The next morning—the opening day of the tournament—dawned cloudless and still. By noon, the heat shimmered over the meadow, and over the hubbub of men's voices, whinnying horses, brawling peasant children and piercing, high-pitched shawms, rose the thin, metallic *tink-a-tink* of the armourer's busy hammer.

Elegantly clad nobles and knights drifted in and out of tents of emerald and rich blue, each bravely flying a knight's colours on banners that hung limp in the heavy afternoon air. Leonor breathed in the smell of dust and perfume, horses and sweat.

Crowds of merchants, musicians, pilgrims, peasants and hawkers of wine and sweetmeats surged behind the double row of sharp-pointed posts sunk into the brown earth. The field itself, enclosed by palisades, was divided by a padded wooden barrier down the centre, high as a horse's shoulder.

Pages serving as water carriers drizzled the straw-covered sand to keep the dust down.

In the centre of the field rose the wooden pavilion dotted with ladies in bright-coloured gowns of fine damask and silk. The brilliant colours swirled together in Leonor's eyes like a multi-hued mosaic.

Squires laced quilted gambesons on their masters, then rolled up the chainmail hauberks and worked them over heads and shoulders. Horses draped in scarlet and green and gold silk whickered and stamped in nervous expectation.

Sitting in the viewing stands next to Jannet and behind the four judges, Leonor blinked away the fine dust that stung her eyes. She was thankful that Reynaud was away from this. Unconsciously she worried her lips raw whenever she thought of him. *He must live. He must!*

At the far end of the tilting yard, the herald, cocky as a popinjay in a red tunic with black silk trim, bawled the identity of each knight as he presented his painted shield to the sound of copper-coloured shawms blasting an ear-splitting fanfare.

'René de Noyon.'

'Gisbert du Clary and his nephew, Jean.'

'Baudoin de Beziers.'

'Bernard de Rodez,' the herald called, his voice growing hoarse. 'Son to Henri, Count of Moyanne and lord of Château Rodez.'

Leonor jolted upright. Because de Rodez had entered the tourney, he would keep himself here, at

Carcassonne, instead of sniffing out Reynaud's destination and riding after him.

Or would he? She shivered, recalling his words. *All the better for what I have in mind for you.*

She shut her eyes and murmured a quick prayer. When she opened them again, the herald had cleared the field for the first event.

The shawms blared. The herald strutted to the centre of the yard. 'Silence!' he shouted. 'The tourney will begin.'

Bernard de Rodez jostled his way to the front of the throng, eager to challenge the other knights.

'Baudoin de Bezier,' the herald shouted. 'Challenger, Bernard de Rodez.'

The horns sounded again and the two knights rode forwards, their mounts kicking up the sand beneath their hooves. The two combatants took positions at opposite ends of the tilt yard, separated from each other by the padded centre barrier. Both were covered in grey chainmail tunics that extended below the knee; their slitted helmets showed only the barest hint of human eyes behind the metal. Leonor strained to make out the devices painted on each man's shield. Were it not for those identifying markings, all the entrants looked alike.

One knight wore a bit of crimson veil pinned to the crest of his helm, showing that he fought for a particular lady.

Leonor watched each knight swear his oath to fight with honour, then take up the lances offered by their attentive squires. She had sat across from

Baudoin de Beziers at table yestereve—a tall, silent man of mature years with an unruly thatch of grey-streaked russet hair. He had seemed self-conscious, had bumped the washing basin when it was presented and had slurped his garlic-and-leek soup. Leonor had noted his obvious discomfort in the company of women and tried to make conversation with him.

Now, the shy man of the evening before looked nothing like this menacing figure clad in grey mail, anonymous but for his sleeveless surcoat marked with the black and gold of Beziers. Leonor shuddered. Brother could fight brother and never know it.

Baudoin de Beziers took up his lance and raised one mailed hand to lower his visor. The crimson veil atop his helm fluttered as he nodded at his squire.

'En joue.'

The horses surged forwards, thundering towards each other on opposite sides of the barrier. At the last moment, each rider raised the blunted tip of his lance and aimed it straight at his opponent.

It was over in a heartbeat. De Beziers tumbled off his horse and lay face down on the ground. His squire darted forwards, followed by a fresh-faced knight, young Jean du Clary.

Leonor guessed the younger man had only recently been knighted; his unscratched spurs still gleamed like new.

'Opponent unhorsed on the first pass,' bellowed the herald. 'Three points awarded to Bernard de Rodez.'

Leonor watched the Hospitaller raise his hand to

acknowledge the cheers of the crowd. De Beziers then limped off the field and the pages darted out with their watering cans.

The scent of damp earth mingled with the flowery perfumes of the ladies and the odour of horses and sweaty men. A sudden chill swept up her backbone. A real fight, such as Reynaud might face, would not smell like a tourney. A real battle would be thick with blood and the stench of death.

She must not think on it. Purposely she focused her gaze on young Jean du Clary. His squire, just a few months younger than the knight he served, was arming Jean for battle, handing him his gloves, then setting the heavy helm over his straight black hair.

The young knight adjusted his visor as the herald marched forwards. 'Jean du Clary challenges Bernard de Rodez.'

The young knight lifted his lance into position. De Rodez did the same.

It was not fair, Leonor thought. Pitting an experienced warrior like de Rodez against a new, untried knight. It broke the unwritten code of fair play governing such events. Perhaps de Rodez would make it easy on the boy.

At the signal, the younger knight dug his spurs into his mount's flanks. The horse jerked forwards. Gathering momentum, du Clary aimed his lance at his opponent's chest. With a crack the dulled point smacked into de Rodez's shield, then slid sideways into his shoulder, pushing him off balance.

The older knight managed to stay in the saddle

while his horse hurtled on, but at the end of the yard, he slumped over and slid to the ground.

A shout went up. The youthful knight rode to the judges' stand, removed his helmet and bowed his head. Leonor noted that his face shone like a fresh-scrubbed boy's. His lips trembled with the effort of not grinning at his triumph.

De Rodez remounted, settling his helmet under one arm while his warhorse danced in obvious anticipation. His lips thinned into a cruel line, and he smiled that odd smile that sent ice through Leonor's veins. He settled the heavy iron helmet over his head and snapped down the nose piece with an ominous click. Then he reached for his lance and spurred the horse forwards, towards Jean du Clary.

Leonor's breath caught. De Rodez had not waited for the herald's signal! Young Jean would be caught off guard, before he could spur his horse. She could not bear to watch.

A shout went up from the onlookers, and she half-rose from the bench and hazarded a glance at the field. Jean du Clary had been unseated. But by the time de Rodez had turned his mount for a second pass, the young knight was on his feet. His squire pressed a sword into his hand just as de Rodez thundered past him, his lance aimed at the boy's heart.

Jean leaped backwards and the lance embedded itself in the hard-packed sand.

Cries of 'foul' filled the air. De Rodez paid no attention. Leonor watched in horror as the bulky Hospitaller wheeled his horse once more and rode straight for du Clary. He was going to run him down!

Just as the horse reached him, Jean jumped to one side. De Rodez jerked hard on his reins, and the great destrier pawed the air. Seizing his chance, Jean fastened both hands around de Rodez's left knee and pulled with all his strength.

Unbalanced, the older knight tipped sideways. Jean grabbed him about the neck and pulled him from his mount.

The crowd cheered.

'Well done!' someone shouted to Leonor's right. Count Roger leaped to his feet and gripped the pavilion railing with both hands. ''Tis within the rules,' he shouted. 'De Rodez is unhorsed!'

The herald made a hurried mark on his roster. 'Three points awarded to Jean du—'

His voice was suddenly drowned out by shouting. 'Look out!' Watch to your left.'

A squire thrust a sword into de Rodez's right hand. With a hoarse cry, he raised it over his head and lunged forwards.

Chapter Eighteen

The sword point caught young Jean du Clary just above the breast bone. De Rodez sliced through the light surcoat and, without the slightest hesitation, pushed the blade into the gap in the chain mail. The sword tip crunched through the hauberk Jean wore underneath.

Du Clary staggered back a step, then sank to his knees, his left hand clasped to his chest. His breathing laboured, he reached his hand to the ground to steady himself. A crimson stain spread where his palm rested.

Gasps arose from the crowd, followed by an uneasy silence. De Rodez's sword had not been blunted, as required by tourney rules.

Jannet's fingers gripped Leonor's arm. '*Pauvre petit,*' she breathed.

'Yield, lad,' Gisbert du Clary called to his nephew from the sidelines. 'Save yourself.'

'Disqualify de Rodez,' someone else shouted. A chorus rose in agreement. 'Penalty! A penalty!'

'Examine his sword.'

'Put him on the barrier!'

'Stop the joust!'

Oblivious, de Rodez stepped forwards and yanked the helmet off the boy's head. 'No one,' he hissed, 'no one unhorses me and lives to brag about it.'

In the sudden hush, his words carried all the way to the judges' stand. Leonor strained to hear the boy's reply.

Jannet leaned towards her husband. 'Roger, you must stop this. De Rodez will kill him.'

'Nay, my love,' the count soothed. 'De Rodez will but teach the boy a lesson.'

'No!' Jannet's eyes flashed as she challenged her husband. 'He will do more than that. I hear it in his voice.'

Count Roger gave her a long look, then turned his gaze towards the field. Raising one hand, he signalled the herald.

A shawm rent the air just as de Rodez set his sword point at the base of du Clary's throat. He forced the young knight backwards until he lay prone, staring with widened eyes at the burly knight looming over him.

The herald's raspy voice grated in the quiet. 'The match is declared—'

Too late. De Rodez thrust his blade home and Jean du Clary's head lolled to one side. Blood gushed from the wound in his neck.

Leonor screamed. This was no tourney! This was purest murder. Then the clamour about her faded, the pavilion's gay colours blurring into a haze. She fancied the plank floor rose to meet her nerveless body, but with a jerk she grabbed the railing and hauled herself upright.

Bernard de Rodez had killed that young knight in cold blood!

Had enjoyed killing him.

The pavilion, the meadow with its coloured tents and gaily caparisoned horses began to revolve about her. She gulped deep mouthfuls of air. When her vision cleared, she began to sweat.

Then she leaned over the railing and retched until she tasted bile in her throat.

Reynaud was right. The world was ugly indeed.

Sickened by the needless death, Leonor fled to the privacy of her chamber with a pounding headache. Inside, she had just thrown herself on the bed when she started at the sight of a figure in one corner of the room.

She bolted upright. 'Benjamin! What are *you* doing here?'

The old man's body unfolded from the single chair, and in an instant she was clasped in his arms, sobbing out the whole story. Benjamin rubbed her back, his bony hand moving up and down between her shoulder blades.

'Hush, little one.'

'Oh, Ben, there is more,' she wept. 'Much more. Reynaud and I…'

'Hush,' Benjamin whispered. 'I know. I am not so old that I have not eyes in my head.'

'And now he has gone on some Templar mission, and I—I fear for his life.'

'What is this mission? Where?'

'I know not. He would not tell me. And that odious man, Bernard de Rodez—'

'Aye. I watched him slay that young knight in the lists just now. I knew how you would feel. I came straight to your chamber.'

'Ben, what should I do?'

'Do? Well, little strong heart, one does what one must. What one can. I understand there is a troubadour competition this evening, and you—'

'I cannot. Not after today. I have no music in me, only darkness.'

Benjamin nodded. 'The world is what it is. Still, it needs music, songs that tell of events we might otherwise forget. The nightingale does not cease to sing on the battlefield, Leonor. It must sing all the louder. That is your dream, is it not? To sing?'

Her head drooped against his chest. 'You are right,' she whispered. 'As always.'

Benjamin tipped her face up and planted his lips on her forehead. 'At last you accept the truth!' he joked. 'Now I must go and search for that young scamp, Galeran. Guard yourself, Leonor. De Rodez is unpredictable.'

When Benjamin stepped outside the door, he stumbled into a round oak tub and four serving maids carrying buckets of hot water. Jannet had sent them.

* * *

Leonor bathed and lay sleepless on her bed until the sun dipped low. Then she rose, listlessly drew on a clean chemise, settled a rose silk gown over it and girdled it at the waist with a linked chain of gold. She went down to supper with an aching heart.

The evening meal was subdued. The knights and ladies of Carcassonne and the nobles from Toulouse assembled quietly at the long trestle tables and ate in silence. Everyone, except for Count Roger, drank too much wine.

Low murmurs of discontent rolled about the hall. Jannet looked inquiringly at the count, but he shook his head. 'Do not concern yourself,' he whispered. 'Such things have happened at tourneys before. While regrettable, no one can be blamed.'

'Not true,' Leonor murmured into Jannet's ear. 'Bernard de Rodez should be blamed. Why does no one accuse him?'

'I know not,' Jannet replied softly.

Leonor stared at her friend. 'This must be how wars start. Some small, ugly incident, like a foolish youth's death, feeds an existing rivalry, and before a year is out, men who were once friends and allies are arming themselves against each other.'

Jannet's dark brows rose. 'Young du Clary's death was needless,' she whispered. 'De Rodez has no concept of honour or the rules of a tourney. He is an animal.'

Leonor gripped her hands together in her lap. Reynaud must not return while de Rodez remained at Carcassonne. She knew of the rivalry between Templars and Hospitallers. If de Rodez pressed his hostility to the breaking point, it would be a fight to the death.

She stared down into her wine cup, numb with grief for the young knight who had been killed and with fear for Reynaud. She did not even hear the herald's first call for the troubadour competition until Jannet gently pressed her arm.

She looked up to see two men step forwards, their instruments slung over their shoulders. How could they even think of singing after du Clary's murder? Her own shaking hands could not hold her harp steady, much less pluck out a tune.

The first harper approached the herald with a swagger. He was dressed in black except for a round gold medallion that hung about his neck on a linked chain, and his shining blond locks fell below his shoulders like a girl's.

From the sighs of the ladies, Leonor guessed he had quite a following. Perhaps he had sung at Great Eleanor's renowned courts of love? If so, she could learn much from him.

'Brian St Clare,' he announced to the herald. 'From the earldom of Orkney.'

His harp, she noted, was strung with silver wire.

The second harper, his brown robe patched and threadbare, looked like a friar from some impoverished monastery. Plump as a ripe peach, the man's ample torso strained the seams of his shabby tunic.

'Andreas is my name,' he announced in a loud,

friendly voice. 'From…nowhere and everywhere, if it pleases my lords. And,' he added with a wink, 'their most fair ladies.'

His fat red cheeks crumpled into a grin. A wandering jongleur! Like as not he would know songs from far-off places. What would he make of her Arab *zajal*?

Jannet pinched her arm and she jumped. Seated, she raised her gaze to the herald. 'I would enter the competition also, with Count Roger's permission.'

The count grinned. 'Granted. I hear she plays like an angel. I will wager twenty gold bezants she walks away with the prize.'

Leonor rose to address the herald. 'I am Leonor de Balenguer y Hassam, my lords. My home is in Granada.'

Murmurs rippled up and down the tables.

'Though I am but a woman, still I would play for Count Roger and his assembled guests.'

'My lady,' a merry voice boomed, 'you look to be lovely enough to grace any man's hall with both music and beauty.' Andreas the harper sent her a flourishy salute, his black eyes twinkling.

'Let her try her hand,' Brian replied with a shrug.

'Accepted,' croaked the herald. He coughed and reached for his wine cup. 'Draw lots, then, to see who will play first.

Leonor selected the shortest straw. She would play last. She gripped her fingers in her lap and listened to the other two harpers.

Too soon it was her turn. Swallows dipped and

swooped in her belly, but slowly she rose to retrieve her harp from its place behind the dais. She surveyed the crowded tables and found the eyes of the diners following her every move. A cold lump of fear congealed in her chest. She raised her chin, looked out over the sea of heads to the doorway at the far wall where a black-robed figure stood.

Benjamin.

Just two songs and she could escape up the stairs to her chamber and be alone with her thoughts. She drew in a long, careful breath. Two songs only. She would make them her best.

Quelling the fluttering in her stomach, she sank on to the low stool and pulled the harp back to rest on her shoulder. *Lord, let my fingers not shake!* She lifted her hands, placed them on the strings and plucked a single, soft chord.

'Hold,' a gruff voice shouted from the back of the hall. 'I challenge the Lady Leonor's right to play for this Christian company.'

Bernard de Rodez strode forwards and tossed his glove down on the floor in front of her.

Chapter Nineteen

Leonor's throat closed over a knot the size of a pomegranate. Count Roger directed a hard look at the brawny knight before him. 'What mean you, de Rodez? Lady Leonor may have lived in Granada, but she is as Christian as you or me.'

'Half-Christian, all Christian, it makes no difference,' de Rodez spat. 'She is damned to hell.'

Trembling, Leonor rose to face him. 'For what offense?'

'Aye, explain yourself,' chorused several voices.

She kept her gaze fastened on Bernard de Rodez's hard, cold eyes. Despite the thumping of her heart, she managed to keep her voice steady.

'For what offence?' she repeated.

Count Roger brought his fist down on the table. 'Out with it, man,' he demanded.

De Rodez merely stared at her for another agonising minute. Then his lips drew back in a chilling smile. 'She is damned to hell for murder.'

Murder! The floor tilted under her feet. She raised her head. ''Tis you who should be accused of murder. This very day I watched you kill that young knight, Jean du Clary. I wonder that you can stand there and accuse another of so foul a deed.'

De Rodez shrugged. 'It was in a tourney. Death often happens so.'

Cries of protest rose.

'Nay!'

'Not so!'

De Rodez lifted one hand and the hall fell silent as a churchyard.

'Hear me. Then you may judge guilt or innocence.'

Her limbs turned into blocks of ice. He had some plot up his sleeve, some lie to tell to draw attention away from his own heinous deed. She was sure of it. Across the room she caught a glimpse of Jannet, staring at the Hospitaller, her face pale as milk.

'Speak, then,' Count Roger shouted. 'And be done with it, so we can get back to our wine and the troubadour competition.'

'I will speak,' the burly knight replied, his rough voice low and menacing. 'This lady, Leonor of Granada, has murdered a child.'

Leonor gasped.

The count leaped to his feet. 'Child? What child?'

'Your son. Galeran.'

Count Roger reeled backwards. 'What did you say?'

'Galeran, my lord. Your son. He is dead. Murdered by the hand of this lady.'

Leonor clenched her fists. 'That is a lie. Galeran was alive and well when last I saw him at the castle in Moyanne. Indeed, he served me most graciously.'

De Rodez pointed a thick finger at her. 'He lives no longer, lady. He was found under a pile of leaves behind his uncle Count Henri's stables.'

A fist closed about her heart and began to squeeze. 'Oh, no. Not Galer—' Her voice broke. 'Surely it is some other boy?'

'It is none else, as you well know. You are guilty of his death.'

'Where is your proof of this, then?'

'I need no proof. The word of a Hospitaller is enough.'

She glanced at Count Roger's stricken face and stiffened her spine. 'I am innocent. I swear it before God and this company.'

Jannet rose and came towards her, but de Rodez blocked her path. 'She stands accused by a knight of a holy order. According to the law, she must prove her innocence. If she cannot…' smiling, he smoothed the sword hilt at his waist '…perhaps the stake?'

'No!' Jannet cried. 'My lord husband—?'

Count Roger passed one large hand over his eyes as if to erase a vision. 'Jannet,' he said, his voice wooden, 'come here to me.'

Jannet hesitated, then stepped towards him. 'My lord, I know you grieve for your son—our son, if you will—but Leonor had naught to do with his death. Do you not remember, she arrived with the Templar some days ago. She could not have…'

'I know,' the count murmured. 'I know. But she stands accused. The law is clear in such a case.'

Jannet gripped both her husband's hands in her own. 'Roger, you cannot do this. It is wrong.'

The count groaned. 'It is the law. She stands accused until proved innocent.'

Leonor began to shake uncontrollably. It had taken only one lie by Bernard de Rodez to change her entire life in a heartbeat. With a flick of his wicked tongue, he had condemned her. How could she ever prove her innocence in the face of such evil?

Dear God, this cannot be happening. None of it is real. Surely she would awaken at any moment to find it was all a terrible dream. *Please, God, please! Let me wake from this nightmare.*

'Death by fire,' the Hospitaller shouted.

'By trial of combat,' a voice spoke.

All heads swivelled to Baudoin de Beziers. 'I will stand for the Lady Leonor,' the tall knight declared. 'Against anyone…' he leveled his steady gaze on Bernard de Rodez '…who accuses her.'

Her heart hammered. Bless the gallant man. Never again, she thought irrationally, would she mind anyone slurping his soup. But Baudoin was no longer young, and he had been badly winded in the lists today. What chance would he have against the Hospitaller?

'Done!' de Rodez snapped. 'Herald, so record it.'

The herald, his jaw agape, jerked to his feet, knocking over his wine cup. 'My lord?' he addressed Count Roger.

The count lifted pain-dulled eyes. 'Yes? What is it?'

'My lord, a trial by combat has been proposed and accepted to establish the innocence or guilt of Lady Leonor in the death of…' He cast a desperate glance around the hall, then gazed down at the table where the wine puddled next to his overturned cup. 'Your son Galeran,' he finished gently. 'Are you agreed?'

The count shuddered. 'I— What was it? Oh, yes. A trial. Yes, I am agreed.' Clutching Jannet's arm, he rose and made his way towards the doorway on unsteady legs.

Leonor wanted to cry out, scream her innocence as the couple moved past her. At the last moment, Jannet met her eyes and gave a barely perceptible nod.

Relief made her knees weak. They knew. They both knew she had nothing to do with Galeran's death.

But someone had. Cold horror swept over her. Who *was* responsible? De Rodez?

Proving her innocence would do nothing to uncover the real murderer. Proving it by combat would simply focus attention on her rather than de Rodez. Either way, whether he won the battle or lost it, that snake would go free.

She was trapped by his guile. She would be sacrificed to cover his own guilt.

Or was there more to his ploy than this? Did his real motive have to do with Reynaud's secret mission? With the rivalry between Hospitaller and Templar for supremacy in France and Spain?

A blade of ice pricked her heart as the realisation dawned. She was the bait to lure Reynaud back to Carcassonne, to be killed.

Chapter Twenty

Reynaud drew back on the reins of his destrier and sat motionless, listening. Over the gusty breathing of the horse, he heard a twig snap. Someone was following him.

Moving very slowly, he dismounted and slapped the horse's rump. Then he stepped noiselessly behind a tree and held his breath until the hoofbeats faded. It was an old trick he used to play on Leonor when they were children.

He closed his eyes. Would that this, too, were only a game.

But it was not. He settled his shoulder against the thick beech trunk and waited. He had circled the château last night, had counted the men positioned as guards along the gated wall. Too many for one man alone. He would not live through this mission.

He thought of Leonor, her warm mouth opening under his, her eyelids damp with tears. How his body ached at the memory.

Yet he had his orders. He must get inside the
château to deliver the gold to a Brother Templar. He
would rather take on a whole troop of Saracen
warriors than penetrate to the core of this well-
guarded château with just his sword and his wits.

Still, there must be a way. He listened intently for
rustling shrubbery or the thump of a horse's hooves
moving on soft ground. Nothing. Whoever followed
him was also adept at the game.

He would wait until nightfall, when his destrier
would circle back to him, then put in motion the
only plan that made sense given the situation. And
pray to God he would survive.

He closed his eyes and thought again of Leonor.
If he lived through this, he would go to her, carry her
off to his bed and do what he had longed to do from
the moment he laid eyes on her—bring her to that
sweet madness that tortured his body and let himself
tumble with her into ecstasy.

He would give up everything, his Templar vows,
his honour—even his sanity—for one night with her.
God knew he was a fool.

But he was a man. And he loved Leonor more than
himself, wanted her more than he had ever wanted
anything. His body burned with it. He did not want to
die now. He wanted to live. To see her again. Touch
her.

Claim her.

When the moon rose, he heard the soft nicker
across the clearing and gave a low whistle. After a

moment the horse bumped his shoulder with its nose. He mounted quietly and walked the destrier forwards with slow, careful steps.

Silhouetted against the moonlit sky, the château rose before him like a huge black confection, all spires and towers, steep slanted roofs and square, smokeless chimneys. Torches burned at the gate-house, the flames guttering in the soft night breeze. Two guards lounged in the archway, playing at pitch-coin. A dozen or more of their companions marched back and forth along the wall walk, talking in low tones.

Reynaud drew rein and listened. No sound emerged from the thick beech woods behind him save for the occasional *tu-whoo* of a night owl. Ahead, the metal coins thudded into the dirt and men laughed. Pigeons gurgled from the dovecote on the roof. He knew its exact location from Brother Pierre's hasty sketch.

He dismounted, lifted one bulging saddlebag on to his shoulder and slapped the horse's hind quarters. The animal jolted away towards the gatehouse, and Reynaud circled to the left, slipping into the shadows at the base of the wall.

One of the guards shouted, *'Un cheval!'* Then the sound of running boots, and a score of armed men poured out through the gate. The horse stood still for a moment, then turned and trotted towards the woods.

The guards hesitated. *'Vite!'* one man hissed. 'Look how that bag behind the saddle bulges. There is some treasure there!'

An argument ensued. While their voices rose,

Reynaud stealthily made his way to the secret doorway at the back side of the wall. Ah, there it was, the narrow gate Brother Pierre had described, hidden beneath a rampant heliotrope vine that drooped over it like a leafy curtain.

He reached out one tentative hand and gave a gentle push. Just as the monk had promised, the latch on the inside had been left unfastened. The plank door creaked open.

Reynaud winced at the sound, waited thirty full breaths before moving forwards. One more push… There!

Again the rusty iron hinge groaned, but by now he could hear the receding shouts of the guards. They had not caught up with the horse, nor discovered the river stones that weighted the remaining saddlebag. The destrier would lead them, little by little, away from their post. Another old trick, this one learned from a captured Saracen.

He stepped through the narrow doorway into a blackness so thick he could not see his outstretched hand. The warm, fetid air smelled sour, and the only sound was the slow drip of water on to stone. Not even the yelling of the guards at the château gate penetrated the unearthly quiet. It was enough to convince him he was entering purgatory.

Without making a sound he withdrew his sword from the belt at his waist, then edged forwards, lifting his leather boots and planting them soundlessly on the hard surface beneath him. A puff of air brushed his face. He jerked his head up and inhaled.

Fresh air, cool and sweet. But coming from where? He moved towards it, one slow step at a time.

The metallic zing of a sword leaving its scabbard cut through the stillness. Without thinking he whirled towards the sound and slashed diagonally upwards from knee to shoulder height.

He heard the sharp intake of breath, then the scrabble of receding footsteps. He waited until the noise faded, then followed in the same direction.

The path slanted sharply downwards, then angled to the right. He reached out one hand and his fingers brushed against damp stone. Probing sideways with his sword, he heard the sharp scrape of steel on rock. A narrow underground passage, he surmised from the dank odour. Not much wider than a large man's body, the ceiling so low his head touched it when he stood upright.

He took care not to graze his saddlebag or the sleeves of his mail hauberk against the sides of the passage. Only once before had he been in such a place—a Saracen dungeon near Edessa. Seventeen days he had spent fighting off rats and thirst before he devised an escape. To stay alive, he had resorted to trapping the rodents at night and eating them raw. His gorge rose at the memory.

A faint silvery light shone ahead of him, and he slowed to a crawl. The passage opened abruptly into a walled garden of some sort, overgrown with scraggly rosemary bushes and rampant tangles of mint.

An instinct made him pause at the tunnel's end,

and in that moment he heard the telltale sound of breathing. Someone waited at the exit to ambush him as he emerged.

He stepped quietly to his right and angled his body until he felt the moist passage wall at his back. He inched forwards until he stood directly by the watcher, his right shoulder almost exposed. Shifting his sword to his left hand, he lunged upwards and slashed to his right.

The blade struck home. A figure tumbled off the overhang and sprawled face down and groaning at his feet. One of the guards.

He waited for the hammering inside his ribcage to subside. How he hated injuring a man, even in battle. But he could ill afford to let the man cry out and warn the other guards.

At the opposite garden wall, a small arched doorway had been cut into the stone. A carved eight-pointed cross, the insignia of the Templars, was incised into the rock. God be praised, at least he would die among brothers. He tramped across the floor of matted thyme and pushed through the entrance.

'Welcome, my son.' From the high-backed chair in the centre of the tiny room, Brother Pierre extended a thin hand. 'You have come swiftly,' the holy man observed.

'So was I ordered.' He stared at the man. Brother Pierre? The narrow face was the same, and the dark, gold-flecked eyes, the voice. But the dirty brown robe and worn leather sandals had been replaced by a chasuble of scarlet silk.

Reynaud scanned the small room. Leaning against the chair was a crosier, the curved head gilded with gold. 'So, it is not Brother Pierre, but *Bishop* Pierre?'

The grey head nodded once. Reynaud studied the unblinking brown eyes of the man seated before him, then let the heavy leather saddlebag slide off his shoulder to the floor at the cleric's feet. 'Here is the gold de Blanquefort promised. There is more, safe in our treasury on Cyprus.'

Bishop Pierre's eyes shone. 'How much more?'

Reynaud hesitated. The treasury contents was privileged information.

'Come, come, Reynaud. Grand Master de Blanquefort and I are old friends. And allies,' he added, lowering his voice. 'What does he offer in exchange for a secret Templar base in Languedoc, a repository under the unwitting protection of King Louis himself? Surely that is worth a fortune?'

Reynaud said nothing. It was not his place to question the dealings of his Grand Master. Or a bishop of the Holy Church. Were they all not united in loyalty to the highest authority of all—Pope Alexander in Rome? And God?

The older man stared down at the gold and thoughtfully stroked his beard. 'A fair bargain. Pope Alexander and the Holy Church will control the Templar treasure in France, and right under the nose of Louis of France, too. With this gold, we will drive the Arab from Spain.'

Nausea cramped his gut.

Without a word, without a backwards glance at Bishop Pierre or the heavy bag of gold at his feet, Reynaud turned away and started for the door.

Chapter Twenty-One

A red-eyed Jannet set the wicker tray of roasted chicken and meat pasties down on the side table in Leonor's chamber. Leonor had spent the whole day in her chamber, had not been able to stop crying and worrying since de Rodez had accused her of murdering Galeran last night. If only Reynaud were here!

Jannet turned to her. *'Mangez, ma petite.* It will do you good.'

'I cannot,' Leonor said in a dull voice. 'How do you fare?'

'Well enough,' Jannet murmured. 'It is Roger who grieves most piteously. I scarcely knew my stepson before he journeyed to Navarre to foster with Roger's brother, your Uncle Henri.'

Leonor drew in a careful breath and slowly lifted a meat pie from the tray, then replaced it. She had no stomach for food. All she could think of was the Hospitaller de Rodez.

'Tell me of the day's tourney,' she begged. 'Anything to take my mind off tomorrow.'

Jannet settled herself on the bed and described each event. 'Bernard de Rodez fought brilliantly, besting every challenger through brute strength and determination.'

Leonor's own champion, Baudoin de Beziers, would meet him in single combat to prove her innocence the following afternoon.

'De Beziers, how did he fare today?'

Jannet's tremulous smile faded. 'Well enough. He has much experience, but he grows old. De Rodez, too, is experienced. But Roger says he fights in blood lust, and that can make a man careless.'

Leonor shuddered. She had seen the Hospitaller's eyes glitter with malevolence, felt his hostility wrap itself around her spirit. There was something unclean about him.

She crossed herself quickly. Surely God would protect her? Proclaim her innocence even against the evil, unleashed fury of Bernard de Rodez?

Jannet embraced her and rose from the bed. 'Roger would be pleased if you will play your harp tonight. It will ease his heartache.' She paused and looked deep into Leonor's eyes. 'You will come down? Men are loath to ask for succour, even when their spirits are in agony.'

Leonor smiled at her friend's earnest entreaty. 'I will.'

'Thank you,' Jannet murmured.

She would go down to the great hall. She wanted

to speak with her champion knight, Baudoin de Beziers, to wish him the best in tomorrow's ordeal. Surely God would not let a good knight like de Beziers die defending her? Yet she did not see how he could overcome so formidable an adversary as the Hospitaller.

Her chest tightened at the memory of Count Roger's stricken face, the bleak, dazed expression that came into his dark eyes when he had learned of his son's death. She pressed her lips together. She must not think on it, must concentrate on the moment at hand and do the only thing she could between now and her trial tomorrow—play her harp.

She would select her songs to ease the soul of the young squire's grieving father and stepmother, and she knew her fellow troubadours, Brian of Orkney and Andreas, would do the same.

Andreas met her when she entered the hall. 'Lady,' he said with a gallant bow. 'The day's greeting to you.' Lifting the harp out of her hands, the pudgy musician guided her to one of the linen-covered side tables. 'Brian and I have saved a place for you between us.' He grinned at his fellow harper.

Brian of Orkney hunched his slim frame over to make room on the bench. 'My lady,' he breathed, a faint smile hovering over the sensitive mouth, 'I am glad you join us this evening. We shall weave a fine web of music.'

He eyed Andreas, who was settling Leonor's harp in a safe corner of the room.

'Andreas,' Brian called to him, his lips twitching. 'Who will play first this evening?'

The bulky harper's eyes looked puzzled for a fleeting instant, then his expression cleared. 'Lady Leonor should play first, followed by you, Master Brian.'

Leonor smiled. Whether by design or accident, Andreas and Brian between them had restored at least some of her spirits. Trial or no, she was not defeated yet.

When at last a lull fell upon the assembled diners, Jannet nodded from the head table, and Leonor rose to retrieve her harp. Seated, she played a virelai she thought would ease Count Roger's heart.

Out of the corner of her eye, she glimpsed a young page skip past her, then slow to a respectful pace as he approached the high table. He whispered into the count's ear, then scampered away.

The count unbent his lanky frame, kissed his wife and left the hall. Leonor sighed. Such were the duties of one born to the manor. The count had not even time for his grief. Distracted, she skipped two verses and finished sooner than she planned.

She drew to a close her second song, about an enchanted nightingale, but Count Roger still had not returned. Whatever it was that detained him must be important, else he would not miss the music he was so fond of.

Her breath caught. Was it about her trial by combat tomorrow? Resolutely she laid the thought aside and concentrated on the final flourish that ended her song.

Next, Brian of Orkney presented two gentle, sweetly sung offerings, and then Andreas followed with an ornamented ballad requiring much skill. His meaty fingers danced over the gut strings, notes tumbled like rippling water, clear and sweet against the darker tone of his voice.

With Andreas's final work, a gay riddle song in triple time that brought a smile to everyone's face, the second evening of the competition drew to a close. Leonor no long cared who won.

She rose to retire, but Jannet signalled to her from across the crowded hall. She waited as the young countess made her way to her side.

'My apologies for Roger's absence,' Jannet began, her melodious voice dropping so that Leonor alone could hear. 'He was called away. Two knights requested the count's presence at the armourer's hut—something about tomorrow's tourney.'

Leonor scarcely heard her words. Her mind buzzed anew with grim thoughts of the coming day. She pressed Jannet's small, warm hand and turned away to seek out Baudoin be Beziers.

'My lord?' she said, lightly touching his shoulder.

The knight bolted off the trestle bench and bowed over her hand. 'Lady Leonor, I bid you good evening.'

'I came to wish you well in the lists tomorrow. And later, in the trial by com—' Her voice choked off. She could not say the word.

Baudoin coughed. 'Fear not, lady. Right will prevail. I will fight to the death on your behalf.'

'I pray it will not come to that, Sir Baudoin. You are a good man, and I would mourn your loss.'

Again Baudoin leaned aside and coughed, and when he met her gaze she glimpsed tears in his eyes. He tried to speak, but could not. Leonor pressed his gnarled hand, turned and fled to the room off the pantry to find Benjamin.

'Now, then, little one,' her old tutor said, awkwardly mopping at her tears with a huge silk handkerchief. 'Tell me.'

'I cannot bear it, Ben. If I should die…'

Benjamin squeezed her shoulder. 'Hush, Lea. You will not die.'

'I would not mind dying so much, it is just…I would never see Reynaud again. And,' she choked out, staring down at her embroidered slippers, 'I do not wish to die in pain.'

'You will not die,' Benjamin said softly. 'Not of unrequited love, and not at the stake for a murder you did not commit. Your champion, de Beziers, is seasoned and tough, never mind his age. Not all old men are as helpless as I feel at this moment.'

She kissed his cheek. 'Thank you for being here with me, Ben. In truth, I am frightened.'

'In truth, little strong heart, you have good cause to be frightened.'

Leonor slipped into the spectators' pavilion and took a seat on the wooden bench next to Jannet. The young woman squeezed her icy hand. 'I pray it goes well for you today.'

'I pray the same,' she murmured. She took a calming breath and looked about her.

The day was hot and cloudless. Sunlight beat down from a sky the colour of brass, and she was grateful for the shade afforded by the multicoloured silk awning over her head. Finches chattered in the branches of the plane trees bordering the lists. Pages passed chilled wine among the noble ladies, who craned their necks in search of this knight or that as they sipped.

In the distance, the piping of a jongleur rose over the general din of preparations. Leonor's heart raced ahead of the rhythm of his tabor and she suppressed a shudder. She downed a sip of the spiced wine and tried to think.

In a few hours her fate—her very life—would be decided by two knights on a field of battle. The skill of two combatants had naught to do with guilt or innocence, but she knew she must submit to the charade of a trial by combat, for that was how Christian law was administered in this land. How different from the ordered practice of law in Granada. Were it not for Reynaud, she wished with all her heart she was gazing on the mountains of her homeland instead of the hills of the world outside.

But there *was* Reynaud. His bronzed, even features, his low voice that moved always on the quiet rivers of her mind. If he were dead, she would feel it in her bones, and a cold, black shadow would shroud her heart.

She looked out beyond the lists to the gold-brown hills and bit into her lower lip. In truth, if Reynaud was killed, she wished to join him in death. The thought of how bleak life would be without him made her stomach clench.

But God alone knew his fate. And hers. Within the hour He would decide whether she lived or died. Seated in a high-backed chair on the other side of Jannet, Count Roger signalled the scarlet-clad herald. With a blare of the shawms, the trial by combat began.

Chapter Twenty-Two

Leonor sat rigid on the bench, arms locked across her rib cage, straining to catch a glimpse of her champion, Baudoin de Beziers. At last, the older knight trotted on to the field just as Bernard de Rodez was accepting a cup of wine from his squire.

'De Beziers is a capable knight,' Count Roger remarked to Jannet under his breath. 'But he is ageing. He fights with skill, yet…'

Leonor flinched. Against de Rodez, Baudoin had little chance. Her throat closed. If her champion lost, would they drag her away and…?

She wrenched her thoughts from the spectre of flames licking at her limbs. *Concentrate on the moment and trust in God.* She lifted her gaze from her trembling knees and came to instant attention.

A hooded figure, a monk by the look of his coarse brown robe, worked his way through the press of on-lookers until he reached the fence enclosing the jousting field.

Another blast of the shawms. 'Single combat,' bellowed the herald. 'Baudoin de Beziers challenges Bernard de Rodez in the matter of charges brought against the Lady Leonor of Granada.'

Leonor entwined her fingers until they ached. Jannet reached out and gave her shoulder a soft squeeze. Desperately she willed her breathing to slow, her heart to cease its hammering.

The Hospitaller mounted and leaned down to take his helmet from the squire. Snapping the nosepiece down over his face, he guided his warhorse on to the field of packed sand where Baudoin de Beziers waited. The wispy burgundy veil Leonor had given him as a token fluttered from the crest of his helmet. At his nod, the two musicians raised their shawms to their lips.

Before they could make a sound, a single rider appeared at the far end of the field, stepping briskly forwards on an unfamiliar dark horse. A dull black metal helmet sat on the broad shoulders, and a plain black surcoat swept down over black chainmail. Even his shield was painted black, and no identifying device was painted on the polished wood.

The herald strode to meet the strange knight. The two men spoke briefly, their voices indistinguishable over the buzzing of curious onlookers. At last, the herald nodded, pivoted and caught Count Roger's eye. A long look passed between the two men. The herald then moved to the centre of the field and raised his hand.

'Will Baudoin de Beziers yield to the Black Knight?'

Baudoin hesitated, then stepped his horse to the pavilion where Leonor sat. He dipped his lance towards Count Roger, then lifted off his helmet and spoke to Leonor.

'My lady, willingly would I fight on your behalf, but another now claims the privilege.' He bowed his head. 'I will yield only to your wishes.'

Tears stung into her eyes at the elderly knight's gallant words. Baudoin was willing to fight—and likely die—for her. And for what? She knew herself to be innocent of de Rodez's charge. But in her heart she knew her ageing champion, however brave, was no match for the Hospitaller.

'Yield to this stranger knight, my lord. My life is in God's hands. If it is to be, I would rather a knight unknown to me die rather than you, whom I know and hold in respect.'

De Beziers saluted her with his lance and, with a final nod at Count Roger, turned his horse towards his sky blue tent at the meadow's edge.

The mysterious Black Knight moved on to the field. The dark warhorse, the plain black high-pommelled saddle and unadorned shield were unfamiliar to Leonor. And to Jannet as well, from the expression her face.

Leonor twisted her fingers together in her lap and darted a glance at Count Roger. Without looking at her, the count signalled a servant, then leaned back in his tall chair to sip his wine, his eyes thoughtful. With his free hand he reached to pat his wife's wrist. 'This should prove interesting, my dear.'

'Interesting!' Jannet raised her eyebrows and leaned towards Leonor. 'Interesting?' she murmured. 'How like a man. For you, it is life and death. For him, it is merely "interesting".'

Leonor's throat was so tight she could not respond. Life and death it was. She wondered how her unknown champion viewed the impending battle—as merely *interesting*? He had put his honour, even his life, at her service. Was it not life and death for him, also?

She studied the figure on the prancing, black-caparisoned steed and saw no sign of fear or even unease. He sat on the horse as still as a statue, not even flicking the reins. Waiting.

The black helmet turned towards her for a brief moment, and behind the narrow eye slits she saw a slight movement. Then the knight raised one mailed hand, saluted her and reined away.

Bernard de Rodez rode on to the field, the rich scarlet of his horse's trapper contrasting with the black surcoat and white cross of the Hospitaller order. His squire, a pudgy lad with a wide leather belt bisecting his fustian tunic, leaned attentively over the wooden fence outlining the field, his eyes avid.

An ear-splitting blast of the shawms rent the air. Before the sound faded, a young page slipped under the fence and sped to the Black Knight's side. Reaching up, he pressed something into the knight's outstretched hand.

Her burgundy veil! Baudoin had sent the unknown knight her favour. Bless the man for such a chivalrous gesture. Dear God, let it bring the stranger knight good luck!

With his own hand, the knight removed his gauntlets and attached the strip of gauzy sarsenet to his helm, then leaned down to speak to the boy. Only now did Leonor note that the Black Knight had not even a squire to attend him. Was he some outlaw knight? A mercenary who fought not for honour, but for ransom?

A chill swept over her. This man did not even know her. Likely he cared not whether his deeds proved her guilty or innocent; a renegade knight who fought for horses and armour and wealth from ransoms. For a fleeting instant she wished her old champion, Baudoin de Beziers, back again.

Ah, no. Her chances were better with the unknown knight, whatever his identity, or his motives, than with a great-hearted but ageing warrior. She drew in a shaky breath and grasped Jannet's hand. 'Truly, you are right, my friend. It is a man's game, in a man's world, is it not? My life seems of small importance.'

Jannet nodded. 'You are frightened,' the young woman murmured, pressing Leonor's icy hands. 'Do not despair, my dear. Roger has grown fond of you. I am sure he will not deal casually with your fate.'

Leonor was not so sure. In her experience men were pragmatic to an extreme. They did what was politically necessary and lived with the consequences.

And Bernard de Rodez? He was a snake.

Why, then, should she trust this nameless knight?

Because you have no choice, a voice reminded. *Because at this hour and in this place, you are but a woman accused.*

She gritted her teeth. And the options open to a woman were defined by… She groaned aloud. Men.

She glanced at Count Roger. He met her gaze, the pain of his son's death barely disguised in his keen blue eyes. Roger was a fair and just man. Though he had suffered a great loss, a loss for which she now stood accused, surely the count would not let her die for something she did not do?

Roger dropped his eyes before her perusal and leaned forwards, intent on the jousting field.

Would he let her die?

The shawms blared again. 'The Black Knight sends a challenge to Bernard de Rodez,' the herald bawled into the still, dusty air. He pivoted and repeated the message once more in each direction to make sure it was heard by all present.

Near the jousting field, Leonor noted, an odd sight was unfolding. A tall, hooded monk left the spectators' ranks and was slowly but deliberately making his way through the crowd to the fenced inner corridor reserved for squires and other retainers. He positioned himself next to the Hospitaller's young squire, then pulled up his hood to hide his face and turned towards the field of battle.

Bernard de Rodez stepped his mount into position, tested the weight of his lance and turned to face his challenger. On the other side of the wooden barrier, the Black Knight sat on his horse without moving a muscle, his lance couched under his arm.

Count Roger raised one hand. The shawms sounded the charge, and de Rodez dug in his spurs. Leonor's chest constricted.

The Black Knight surged towards him, keeping his lance up. At the last moment, he aimed the tip at the Hospitaller's helmet.

The Black Knight's lance shattered. As de Rodez thundered past, he wheeled his horse and quickly repositioned himself. But now he was without a weapon.

Leonor's heartbeat tripled. With no squire to serve him, no attendant of any kind, the unknown knight would be unable to re-arm himself.

But, no! A knight rode forwards from the sidelines and offered his own lance. She recognized Baudoin de Beziers.

Another shawm blast, another charge. The two opponents again spurred their warhorses towards each other, and Roger gulped his wine.

This time the Black Knight struck de Rodez's shield with such force that he reeled in the saddle.

Count Roger grunted. 'One strike each.' He tipped his head towards Jannet. 'That one is no stranger to battle,' he remarked in an undertone.

'Which one do you mean, husband?'

His eyes riveted on the field, the count did not answer.

Jannet caught Leonor's gaze and rolled her eyes skyward. *Les hommes!* she mouthed. *Quel mal de tête!*

Both knights repositioned themselves and signalled their readiness. The shawm players raised
their horns. Leonor shut her eyes. *Please, let the
stranger knight not be defeated!*

At the clash of impact, her lids flew open.

Both lances had snapped. De Rodez dismounted
immediately and strode towards his squire. The lad
advanced, holding out a two-edged sword.

Leonor held her breath. The Black Knight had
neither sword nor attendant. She watched him turn
his horse towards the spectators' gallery and raise
both hands, showing that they were empty. Then he
dismounted and moved purposefully towards de
Rodez's squire.

No, towards the tall monk!

From under his robe, the hooded figure produced
a fine sword, its hilt encrusted with crimson gems.
The stranger knight stepped forwards and lifted it out
of the monk's hands.

A gasp went up from the crowd. Was the sword
known to some of the onlookers? Leonor squinted
her eyes to get a good look at the weapon.

She had never seen one like it before.

A cry went up from the knights of Toulouse,
bunched together at one end of the field. They recognised the sword! Was her champion then one of
them? A knight of Toulouse?

She racked her brain to recall their faces. None
she remembered were as tall as the Black Knight.

The herald lifted his arm for silence, and the field
quieted. 'Combat will continue with swords. And,'

he added, drawing a tired breath, 'because this trial shall be settled by force of arms, combat shall continue...' he paused for a split second and caught Count Roger's eye '...to the death.'

A great roar went up. Jannet clutched her husband's arm. 'Roger, you cannot. You—'

He turned an impassive face towards his wife. 'An eye for an eye,' he muttered.

Leonor froze. He could not mean it. Surely one death, even if it was his own son, could not mean...

But he did mean it. She could see it in his face. Her stomach roiled. She remembered how Bernard de Rodez had killed young Jean du Clary on the first day of the tournament, the vicious pleasure on his face as he drove his sword into the young knight's throat.

How de Rodez loved killing! Such a man did not fight like other men. He fought like one possessed of a demon. A blade of ice pressed into her heart. If de Rodez succeeded in killing the Black Knight, she would die as well.

She knotted her fingers in her lap and looked to the field. Before her horrified eyes, Bernard de Rodez lunged at the stranger knight, slashing the black surcoat to tatters and striking the mail tunic underneath with a metallic clank.

The Black Knight twisted away to avoid a second blow, then swiftly thrust his sword upwards. The blow glanced off the Hospitaller's shield. The two men crouched, circling each other, looking for an opening.

The Black Knight struck first. The blow knocked de Rodez backwards, but he regained his balance. Dropping his shield, he grasped his sword hilt in both hands and swung the blade sideways in a deadly arc.

The stranger knight jumped aside, but not soon enough. The blade bit into the metal links under his left arm.

Leonor winced. The blow hurt, for the man clapped his arm tight against his body, but he made no sound. He stepped neatly to one side, then sprang forwards, his own sword gripped in both hands.

Now neither man had a shield! It could not last long. Unable to look away, she clenched her fists in mounting terror.

The Black Knight sliced his weapon through the air with such speed it made a faint whoosh. The tip ripped into the mail over the Hospitaller's chest. His breath came in great throaty gasps, and the rhythm now grew uneven.

Leonor dug her nails into her palms. De Rodez was tiring.

But not enough. He was a strong fighter, and well seasoned. It would not be easy to best him. As for killing him… She had seen no man capable of that since the tourney began. Even now he rallied, blocked the stranger's sword thrust and moved adroitly out of range.

Both men gasped for air, their breath gusting in and out behind the metal headpieces. She saw the cold glitter of de Rodez's eyes behind the slitted opening in his helm, and a shadow slid over her heart.

Abruptly the Black Knight whipped his blade upwards, knocking the Hospitaller's helmet off his head. De Rodez fell backwards and the metal headpiece rolled to one side. In an instant, the Black Knight straddled him, his sword poised at his throat.

'Yield,' he demanded.

'Never,' de Rodez shouted. Lifting his sword arm, he slammed the flat side of his blade into the back of the Black Knight's right knee, unbalancing him.

Count Roger sucked in a sudden gasp. 'De Rodez fights by no rules save his own,' he muttered.

The Hospitaller kicked upwards with one foot, landing a crunching blow to the Black Knight's groin. He buckled, tried to straighten, but the Hospitaller scrambled to his feet.

The crowd buzzed like a horde of angry wasps. 'Fight fair,' a voice shouted. Leonor recognized the burly labourer who had greeted them on their arrival at Carcassonne.

Now the unknown knight began to stalk de Rodez. Around the entire tourney field they went, feinting, circling, landing an occasional blow. Both were bleeding, gulping air in hoarse, raspy mouthfuls.

Suddenly de Rodez launched himself at the Black Knight, knocking him to his knees. In the next instant, he raised his sword in both hands and smashed it against the Black Knight's helmet. The knight fell forwards, and the metal helm clattered on to the sand. De Rodez raised his sword, aimed it at the knight's unprotected neck.

Leonor cried out in disbelief. Was a fight to the death conducted without honour? Sickened, she turned her head to one side and fought back nausea.

The Hospitaller drove his blade downwards, and the crowd screamed.

Chapter Twenty-Three

A cheer burst from the spectators' pavilion, and, in spite of her horror, Leonor turned back to the field, her throat tight. The Black Knight had rolled away at the last moment. Now, he grasped his sword and raised his uncovered head.

Reynaud!

Her vision blurred, then dimmed. Surely she was dreaming.

Reynaud pulled himself painfully to his feet and stood, swaying, his sword clenched in his right hand.

'So, Templar,' de Rodez rasped. 'We meet again.'

To conserve his strength, Reynaud said nothing. He watched the Hospitaller circle him, studying the man's movements for a weakness, a misstep, keeping his sword ready to strike. De Rodez was built like a boar, his body compact. His keen eye missed nothing. Every move Reynaud made was tracked and assessed and countermanded. More than that, he deduced from de Rodez's arrogant stance, the man was used to winning.

He saw an opening, and his blade flashed. De Rodez spun out of range and the blow glanced off his mailed shoulder. The burly knight lunged back towards Reynaud's unprotected left side, and only at the last instant did he manage to leap clear.

'No man has ever bested me, Templar,' the knight grated, his voice hoarse with fury. 'No one.'

Reynaud smiled into the mottled face. 'Count not your eggs until you have caught the hen.' He feinted to the right to avoid a blow. 'And the rooster, as well.'

He flicked his sword tip against the butt of the Hospitaller's elbow, an old Saracen trick. Instantly de Rodez's fingers opened in reflexive action and his sword thudded on to the ground.

Reynaud bent to retrieve it, and an expectant hush fell over the crowd. Reynaud watched his opponent and waited.

The Hospitaller's eyes narrowed into molten slits. He opened his mouth to speak, but no sound came forth.

Again he smiled. That was the key, then. De Rodez's weakness was his unreasoning anger. Reynaud advanced a step and held out the knight's sword, hilt first.

'Take it. I cannot kill you unarmed.'

De Rodez made a low growling sound in his throat, but did not move.

'I do not ask you to beg,' Reynaud said in a quiet voice. 'Why do you hesitate?'

But he knew why. It was one thing to be beaten on the field of honour, quite another to be humiliated before his peers. The cold glitter in the Hospitaller's eyes told him he had succeeded not only in unhanding his enemy, but in unmanning him as well. Now, driven by blind rage, his opponent would fight like a cornered animal.

And, Reynaud prayed, he would fight unwisely.

Before he had completed the thought, de Rodez snatched up his sword and threw himself forwards, thrusting wildly with the steel blade. Reynaud side-stepped, dodged, twisted to left and right. Then the Hospitaller stopped for an instant to catch his breath, and Reynaud saw his chance.

His blade caught de Rodez under his armpit.

The man screamed in fury and lunged forwards, raining uncontrolled blows like thunderbolts. One sideways slice penetrated the mail near Reynaud's shoulder, driving the metal links through the quilted gambeson and into his flesh. His skin burned. Blood soaked the neck of the protective undergarment. Tomorrow, he would be more than bruised and aching.

If God let him live until tomorrow. He was cut at the neck and shoulder, though he knew not how deep the wounds were. How much longer could he last?

De Rodez fought like a berserker, not for honour. Not even to prove his charge against Leonor, but for revenge. He kept pressing forwards, pressing closer with the instinctive cunning of a predator.

Reynaud saw that he might have to kill him after all.

He let the bulky knight slowly drive him backwards, towards the fence, all the while watching for an opening. The Hospitaller's harsh breath pulled in and out in a ragged rhythm.

Reynaud concentrated on moving very little, garnering what strength he had left for the single blow he would need to bring the man down.

The Hospitaller lunged wildly and missed. With a single-minded surge of will, Reynaud lifted his sagging sword arm and struck a blow to his opponent's chest that toppled him on to his back. Quickly he moved to stand over the man and pressed the tip of his sword into the exposed throat.

'Yield.'

De Rodez's lips drew back in a snarl. 'Never.'

'Then you will die to prove what you already know.' He nicked the ruddy skin beneath his blade. 'The Lady Leonor is innocent of murder. Say it.'

De Rodez stared up at him, his eyes like two black stones.

Reynaud let the weight of his sword force the wound deeper. A crimson bubble of blood bathed the steel. 'Say she is innocent, and I will spare you.'

De Rodez sucked in a lungful of the dusty air and closed his eyes. 'I—I would live.'

Reynaud chuckled. 'Speak, then, so all can hear. Say that Leonor is innocent.' He nudged the Hospitaller with his boot. 'Say it!'

The knight's lips opened. 'She is…not guilty,' he muttered. 'Not guilty.'

Leonor's knees turned to water. Trembling, she

sank on to the bench. Without a word, Jannet lifted the cup of wine out of her husband's grasp and held it to Leonor's lips.

'Drink. It is not watered and will restore you. You are white as a shroud.'

She took the wine from Jannet's hand and gulped the rich liquid. She swallowed another mouthful, then another, and handed the empty goblet back to Count Roger.

When the count reached to accept it, his hand shook so violently he could not grasp the cup.

'My lady, if you please.' A young page in a green tunic tugged at her skirt. 'The Black Knight wishes to speak to you. He lies in yon tent.' The boy pointed a small hand at the dark blue pavilion flying a crimson banner. Bernard de Bezier's tent.

She overtook the page and brushed past the man-at-arms stationed outside. Inside the tent it was dim and cool, the air heavy with the smell of sweat and camphor.

'Where is he?'

'Here,' a gravelly voice called from behind a curtain. A frowning Baudoin de Beziers pulled the drape aside.

Reynaud lay on a cot, his face white. Benjamin bent over him, a blood-soaked towel in his hand.

'Do not talk!' he snapped. He pressed a fresh towel to Reynaud's neck.

'I must,' Reynaud said.

It was an effort for him to speak. Quickly Leonor moved to his side and laid her fingers against his lips.

Benjamin replaced yet another crimson-stained towel, and Reynaud's mouth twisted in pain.

'Do not speak, Rey. Lie still.'

'I cannot stop the bleeding,' Benjamin muttered.

Reynaud's eyelids fluttered closer. 'I am dying, then?'

'No!' Leonor shouted the word. 'Do you hear me? You are not to die!'

'Perhaps,' Benjamin muttered. 'Keep him quiet while I stitch up this gash. Missed an artery by a hair.' The old man signalled her to press hard on the towel at Reynaud's neck while he scrabbled in his medicine bag for needle and silk stitching thread.

'I must speak, Lea. My vision grows darker.'

'Shut the man up!' Benjamin ordered. He jabbed a silver needle into the skin next to the gaping wound and tugged the silk tight. Reynaud hissed in air, but did not move.

Another jab and the backs of her eyelids began to sting. With the third stitch, Reynaud opened his eyes.

'Wine,' he croaked.

'And poppy juice,' Benjamin ordered. 'There, in that vial.'

De Beziers spoke to a servant and at once a cup of dark liquid appeared. She poured in the contents of the vial.

'He cannot raise his head to drink,' Benjamin said. 'Drip it into his mouth, if you can find a way.'

She reached under her damask gown and tore a strip from her linen chemise just as de Beziers appeared with another cup of wine.

'For you, my lady. You look more pasty than buttermilk.'

He set the cup down on the table next to Benjamin's black leather bag, took one look at the pile of blood-soaked towels accumulating on the tent floor, and shouted for the servant.

Leonor dipped the linen strip into the doctored wine, and when it was sopping she squeezed it over Reynaud's open mouth.

'More,' Benjamin ordered, still bent over his stitching.

She gulped a mouthful of her own wine, sent de Beziers a nod of thanks, and dribbled more of the poppy-laced liquor past Reynaud's lips.

After a time his breathing grew less laboured. He swallowed another dose of drugged wine, then startled her with a question.

'What think you of the world outside Granada now?'

His inquiry sliced to ribbons what had been her childishly innocent view of life in the wider world. She understood now why Reynaud had opposed her undertaking.

'It is more…more everything. More surprising. More exciting. More brutal and frightening than I had ever dreamed.'

A chuckle erupted from Reynaud's throat. Benjamin lifted his needle and swore under his breath.

She gazed into Reynaud's sea-green eyes, noting the pain and hunger, and the weariness.

'And at the same time,' she murmured, 'the world is more beautiful than I had thought.' She laid her hand lightly on his bare chest. Beneath her fingers she felt the unsteady thump of his heart.

Gently he covered her hand with his own. 'Such education costs dearly,' he murmured. 'It can scar your soul with such blackness you can never find your way back.

'That I now know,' she whispered. 'I will never forget.'

Benjamin cleared his throat and poked the needle in for another stitch. Reynaud winced, then lifted his hand from hers and brought it up to touch her face. 'I would keep you safe, Lea. Protect you from all that is evil and dangerous.'

'You know you cannot, Rey. You cannot be with me always. I must learn to protect myself.'

He groaned and shook his head. 'I knew you would say that.'

'And what of you? In your eyes I see two things— anguish and hunger. You are scarred, Rey. You must find some joy in this world to soften your distress.'

Reynaud hesitated. Aye, he had discovered joy. Being near her, hearing her voice, admiring her wit, her courage. Even her stubbornness. Watching her sing those exquisite melodies that caught at his heart and ensnared his soul.

Wanting her.

What saved him from despair was his unspoken bond with her.

'There is joy in serving God,' he said. 'In fighting

for what is good and true. In fulfilling my duty to the Templar brotherhood.'

She bent forwards, her warm breath washing against his chin. 'Is there room for nothing more?'

'I do not know,' he said in an undertone.

'Do you wish for more?'

'Aye.'

Benjamin tugged the last stitch tight and Reynaud ground his teeth. 'I vowed to dedicate my life to the Templars, but that was before I returned to Granada. Before I saw you again. Before I realised what I have longed for all my life.'

'Tell me,' she whispered.

'I want…to be with another human being. I want to be with you, Lea. You are the only music my heart has ever known.'

Benjamin grunted over his final silk knot, reached for Leonor's wine cup and drained it in three swallows.

'You can talk now,' he grumbled to Reynaud. 'But if you move even one finger, you will spoil my stitches. Do you understand me?'

Reynaud did not answer.

Leonor lifted her head, her eyes brimming. 'He understands you, Ben. He understands…everything.'

Chapter Twenty-Four

At supper that evening Leonor nodded at Baudoin de Beziers's solemn-faced gesture of invitation and sat down next to him at the long trestle table, pulling her pale green damask gown out of the path of the knight's huge feet. A meal with the taciturn de Beziers for a supper partner appealed to her. Reynaud was still recovering in Baudoin's tent, and she had no stomach for pleasant chatter.

Her knees were still quivery, but an odd feeling of euphoria made her lightheaded. *You are the only music my heart has ever known.*

She drew in a shuddery breath; without a word, Baudoin filled her wine cup and offered her a choice piece of roast capon. Perhaps he understood her need for quiet after such a tumultuous day. The silver-haired knight bent his head towards her.

'Look to your left, lady,' he murmured. 'And beware. The Hospitaller still smarts from his wounds.'

Leonor scanned the room full of noisy diners until she recognised de Rodez's green surcoat. Cold blue eyes hard as agate stared back at her. A chill wound up her spine, prickling her scalp under the gold band that secured her veil. She laid her eating knife beside the trencher.

'I fear him, even now,' she whispered.

Baudoin grunted and speared a morsel of capon with his blade. 'I trust he is unarmed. Count Roger does not allow swords at table.'

'Still,' she added quietly, picking up her knife, 'that one is dangerous, sword or no sword.'

'Aye. Reynaud must take care.'

She jerked and her eating knife clattered on to the trencher.

'The Templar,' Baudoin said as if reading her thought, 'is well guarded in my tent. The physician, Benjamin, tends him as well.'

Baudoin scraped the pungent sauce off the capon and cut it into two portions. 'Eat, lady. It may be a long night.' He laid a portion on to her plate.

She studied the impassive face of the lean knight at her side. Baudoin knew more than he was saying. In her bones she knew he was warning her of danger.

'I will take note of that,' she murmured.

The older knight shot her a quick, appraising look and grunted, pointing with his knife at her untouched supper.

'And I will eat…' she flashed him a wavering smile '…as you order.'

De Beziers stared down at his sauce-smeared

plate. 'You are obedient, lady. A trait rare in one so—' He broke off. Colour flooded the skin above his silver-tinged beard.

'In truth, I am not obedient, good Baudoin,' she whispered. 'It is my worst fault. I eat because it is sensible to do so.'

The knight trained amused grey eyes on her.

'Tonight,' she explained, 'we—the harper Andreas and Brian of Orkney and myself—will each offer one final song for the judges. I cannot sing on a empty stomach.'

Baudoin nodded. 'Just so.'

'They, however…' Leonor gestured down the long table where Andreas and Brian hunched over their shared trencher '…can sing whether stuffed or starving. Such is the uncertain life of a troubadour, they tell me. They usually eat the sweetmeats first, I notice.'

De Beziers's lips twitched into a rare smile. 'Not only are you beautiful, lady, you are observant as well.' Blushing scarlet at his own audacity, he ducked his head and stared into his wine cup.

She resisted the impulse to gently tease the gallant old man. Like as not it would embarrass him, and from the look on his face he was uncomfortable enough. She tipped her head towards him and spoke under her breath.

'I am alive this night, Sir Baudoin, and that makes me notice and savour each small thing I see. I give thanks that my eyes are open and not lidded with death coins, that my flesh craves sustenance to go on living. And,' she added more softly, 'that you spoke for me, as my champion.'

De Beziers nodded. 'I spoke. The Templar fought.'

'Nonetheless, I am grateful. The song I will sing tonight is for you.'

The knight raised his head. As she watched, the grey eyes filled with tears. Slowly he lifted her hand to his lips. 'Much is lost when one grows old.'

Her heart squeezed. Thanks to Baudoin, she was alive and hungry for life. Mayhap in days past he had felt the same.

Her body throbbed with awareness. Her blood sang. But it was Reynaud she longed for. She hoped Baudoin in his youth had also loved someone. One should not leave this life without knowing, at least once, the peace of another's touch upon one's soul.

Today she had faced death. Tonight she wanted to revel in life. She wanted Reynaud. Now. Tonight. Her veins burned with it. *Let him be well. Let him come to me…take me, before I die of desire. Ah, I will never again feel truly alive without him.*

Later, Leonor rested her harp against her shoulder and let her voice rise and float out over the great hall. She sang for Baudoin de Beziers, for youth left behind. For Count Roger and the loss of his son. And for Reynaud. What a precious gift God gave when He breathed life into a man.

A hand gripped her shoulder so hard the harp teetered in her lap. 'Cease!' a voice cracked.

Bernard de Rodez loomed before her, his face

crimson, his breathing ragged. She shrank away, but his fingers bit into her flesh.

Over his shoulder she glimpsed Count Roger, half-risen from his chair, his face pale but for the jagged purple scar tracing a line across his cheek. Beside him at the high table, Jannet laid her hand on her husband's arm, then rose quietly and moved towards the kitchen.

'Do not play so sweet a song, lady,' de Rodez hissed. 'It grates upon me.' A strange light shone in the Hospitaller's eyes, like the black, unblinking gaze of a falcon trained on a morsel of meat.

Her blood turned cold. Without thinking she made a hurried sign of the cross over her breast.

'God will not help you,' de Rodez thundered. 'Nay, lady, you will burn in hell for what you have done.'

She struggled to control her voice. 'I have done nothing. And so it was proved this day by trial of combat. I am innocent of your charges. My champion's sword proved this to be so.'

'You are a woman,' he snorted. 'A woman is never "innocent", no matter what a sword decides.'

He was mad, she realised. And dangerous. That was what Baudoin had tried to warn her about Bernard de Rodez. He had gone out of his wits.

Very gradually she let her harp slide down until it touched the floor. Then she rose to her feet, flinching as his hand crushed her shoulder.

'It is not the sword that proves my innocence. It is my own word and deed. By your own admission, no longer do I stand accused.'

'Nevertheless,' de Rodez breathed, 'I am not finished with you. Not yet.'

Leonor's limbs turned to wood.

'Ah, but you are indeed finished,' a voice rang from the back of the hall.

Benjamin! What was he doing here? Why was he not tending Reynaud's wounds?

The Hospitaller whirled. His sword scraped as he slid it from the belt hidden under his surcoat. Benjamin's black-robed figure moved forwards.

'You cannot kill me before I have spoken,' the old man called. 'And speak I will, if this company will allow me to tell a truth.'

'Tell! Tell! Let him speak,' a hundred voices echoed about the hushed room. From the corner of her eye, she watched Benjamin advance another unsteady step.

'You are armed,' Benjamin observed. 'I had thought swords were not permitted at Count Roger's table.'

More murmurs from the assembled diners.

'But,' Benjamin's penetrating voice continued, 'perhaps you have your reasons?'

De Rodez shrugged. Benjamin moved another step towards him. 'I would arm myself also, were I you and the truth were known.'

'Truth?' the Hospitaller rasped. 'What would an old man know of truth?'

'A great deal, I fear. About young Galeran, the count's son.'

At the mention of his son's name, Count Roger made a muffled sound and started towards de Rodez. 'What about my son?'

Benjamin shifted his black eyes towards the count. 'Galeran has been missing from Castle Moyanne these many days. Ran away to Carcassonne, so we thought. To his father, Count Roger. At least that is what all at Moyanne believe.'

De Rodez went suddenly rigid.

'But that is not so, is it, Bernard de Rodez?'

Speechless the Hospitaller confronted the old man. Benjamin's voice rose in a battle cry. *'Is it?'*

Leonor stared at the two men. Benjamin took another step forwards. *Mother Mary, he must stop! De Rodez will kill him!*

'You accused the Lady Leonor of murder.' Benjamin's voice rang against the stone walls. 'You insisted the boy was buried near Castle Moyanne, under a pile of leaves in back of the stables, you said.'

De Rodez's sword arm twitched.

Benjamin stepped between the Hospitaller and Leonor, drawing de Rodez's sword to himself. 'How,' he pursued, 'did you know that to be true, eh?'

De Rodez remained silent.

'It *is* true,' Benjamin continued. He turned his head towards Count Roger. 'There was an eyewitness to the deed.'

Cries of outrage rose from the horrified onlookers.

'There was no witness,' de Rodez snarled.

Benjamin pinned the knight with his sharp, black eyes. 'There was. I discovered it only this afternoon, during the trial by combat.'

De Rodez scowled at him. 'Where is this witness, then?'

Benjamin chuckled. 'Here with me now, at Carcassonne. Hiding under a pallet, quaking in fear.'

A muffled groan drew Leonor's gaze to the back of the hall where a small robed figure stiffened against the stone wall.

Benjamin's voice carried over the buzz of questions. 'And now the witness will speak.'

Chapter Twenty-Five

'Tell them!' Benjamin called over his shoulder to the motionless figure huddled near the kitchen entrance. 'Tell them what happened at Castle Moyanne.'

Silence. Benjamin's brilliant black eyes held those of the Hospitaller. 'Say what you know of this man, Bernard de Rodez.'

A quickly indrawn breath broke the hush in the hall, but no one spoke.

'Come forwards,' Benjamin called. 'Speak the truth, as you spoke it to me this very afternoon.'

A small pale face appeared in the light flickering from the candle sconces along the wall, the visage seeming to float above the dark robe.

Galeran! The young squire looked like a frightened hare caught in a willow trap. Count Roger stumbled in his haste to reach the boy, caught the small figure up in his arms and buried his face against his son's neck.

Benjamin raised his voice. 'Galeran, I know you fear Bernard de Rodez's sword if you reveal what you know. But so help me, if you do not speak, and soon, I will save the Hospitaller the trouble and thrash you myself!'

The small figure jerked. 'W-what shall I say, Benjamin? About the ditch, or—' He snuggled his face against his father's broad shoulder.

'Tell them,' Benjamin said through gritted teeth, 'about what Bernard de Rodez did to you.'

Silence fell, so prolonged Leonor thought she would scream. Benjamin moved a step closer, positioning himself within range of the blade, yet too close for the powerfully built knight to manoeuvre for a thrust. The Hospitaller gripped his sword hilt with both hands, his arms trembling.

'He…' Galeran's high, thin voice wailed. 'He… That man, the Hospitaller, he put his hands about my throat and choked me until I could not breathe, and…and then everything went dark. I woke up under a pile of leaves in the ditch behind the stables.'

'The boy lies!' de Rodez barked. 'I know naught of this. It is but the rambling of a foolish lad, and I will kill any who say otherwise.'

Leonor took a step forwards. 'Then you will have to kill me, as well, since it was you who falsely accused me of this deed. You described the very grave in which Galeran lay. Only one who laid him there could have known of it, de Rodez. You have given yourself away.'

De Rodez's eyes widened, filmy and unfocused. '*He* did it. The Jew.'

'Nay, he did not,' she replied, her voice trembling. 'You did it.'

Murmurs rose from the diners who crowded forwards. Benches scraped, tables were vacated as the men retrieved weapons hung from hooks embedded in the stone wall. A grim Baudoin de Beziers buckled on his sword belt. The knights of Toulouse gathered in a knot at one end of the hall. One by one, they turned towards Bernard de Rodez.

Oh, no, not more bloodshed? Horrified, she caught Benjamin's eye. An almost imperceptible shake of his head told her what she wanted to know. Benjamin would press for the truth, but would not compromise the boy's safety.

The ominous quiet stretched until the only sounds were the rough breathing of every man in the hall and the thrum of her own heartbeat. Tension sizzled until she could smell it, sharp and yeasty. The smell of fear.

The fine hair on her forearms lifted. She had to do something, anything, to break the thick silence. In desperation, she looked to Count Roger. The count stared back at her with anguished eyes, his face white as ground oats. A moment passed, then two. No one moved, as if a spell had been cast over the entire hall.

Bernard de Rodez's strange, cold eyes held hers, the dark pupils dilated, a hot, malevolent light kindling in their depths. Without moving a muscle, he spoke. 'I will destroy any who speak against me. Even you, lady.' His beefy hand tightened about his sword hilt.

She swallowed hard. 'You will never destroy the truth, Bernard de Rodez. You must live with it, always. And die with it staining your soul.'

'That I will not,' he shouted. His left hand shot out, pinning her wrist. He jerked her forwards and savagely twisted her arm behind her back. Pain shot through her shoulder. She bit her lip to keep from crying out.

The Hospitaller moved forwards a step, propelling her ahead of him as a shield, gesturing with his sword to clear a path.

What could he hope to do in a hall full of armed knights? She stumbled over an uneven plank in the floor. De Rodez dragged her upright and she yelped in agony.

In the next instant a man stepped from the shadows, his sword drawn. 'Release her!'

Reynaud! A thick pad of towelling was tied around his neck and one shoulder. Dark bloodstains marked his tunic. He strode towards her, the garnet-studded hilt of his weapon gleaming in the candle-light. Whispers circled the hall like wind among dry leaves.

'That sword!' someone called out. 'It was the sword of Arnaud of Toulouse!'

Behind her another voice shouted and Benjamin moved forwards, his dagger drawn. '*Manus haec inimica tyrannis!*' he intoned to Reynaud. She groaned aloud. Benjamin's small knife would be useless against de Rodez's heavy double-edged sword.

'*Macte!*' Reynaud answered.

The Hospitaller yanked hard on her arm. 'Move, damn you!'

She closed her eyes against the bolt of pain that stabbed between her shoulder blades. 'Nay,' she gasped. 'I will not.'

Then Reynaud was before them, his face pale, but his blade flashing, searching for an opening between her torso and de Rodez's bulky form. Instinctively she tried to twist to one side, but de Rodez wrenched her arm so hard her knees buckled.

'Release her!' Reynaud's voice rang like hardened steel. 'Then, dog of a dog, you will face me like a man.'

Instead, de Rodez pulled her in front of him, forcing her body to protect his. White-hot pain knifed through her shoulder socket, and with a cry she flung herself to the right.

Reynaud launched himself towards de Rodez, but the Hospitaller thrust his sword tip past her shoulder, slicing into Reynaud's chest. Blood welled through the fabric of his tunic.

Reynaud smashed his rigid hand against de Rodez's throat, breaking his grip on Leonor. She sagged towards him. He pivoted, caught her shoulder with his free hand and dragged her out of sword range.

A scream of rage broke from de Rodez. He grasped his sword with both hands and raised it over his head, his gaze intent on Reynaud's unprotected back.

Someone moved forwards. 'Rey!'

Too late. De Rodez's blade struck Reynaud's wounded shoulder.

Shouts of outrage echoed through the hall. With a hoarse cry, Reynaud released her. Shoving her behind him, he turned to face his opponent, his injured sword arm drooping.

With an animal-like growl, de Rodez again seized his weapon in both hands. He took his time, aiming carefully at Reynaud's bare neck above the blood-stained tunic. Leonor willed herself not to scream. Such a blow would take his head off.

She threw herself towards de Rodez.

Reynaud shouted a war cry, slapped his sword into his left hand and lunged forwards. His blade caught de Rodez's exposed throat and drove through the flesh. With a gurgling sound, the Hospitaller pitched forwards and lay still.

Reynaud stood over the unmoving form, his chest heaving. Sweat poured down his face, dripped on to his tunic. He wiped his sleeve across his forehead and a tumult of shouts erupted.

'Leonor.' His hoarse voice caught. 'My sword is recognised. Toulouse harbours no love for its bearer, and I must flee. Meet me—'

'No! I will come with you.'

He groaned. 'There is not time.'

She caught his gaze and held it. His eyes looked weary, full of pain. Her heart twisted. By sheer force of will she stifled the sob that closed her throat.

'There is time.'

Baudoin de Beziers, his sword clamped in his grip,

strode to Reynaud and shoved him towards the doorway. 'Ride away, Templar, before these Toulouse upstarts slaughter you. And your lady, as well.'

Reynaud nodded. The anguish she saw in his green eyes tore at her insides. Behind her a sword scraped out of its scabbard and at once a dozen knights surged towards Reynaud. He must abandon her or be killed.

Baudoin de Beziers's brusque voice spoke at her elbow. 'Get you gone, lady!' He raised his sword and turned towards the advancing knights, speaking to her over his shoulder. 'Fly with him, Leonor, else he will not leave. Saddled horses wait in the yard. Take them and go!'

Before she could reply, a blade flashed. Deftly, Baudoin blocked the blow. 'Go!' he ordered. 'Up the stairs. There is a passage. He knows of it.'

He broke off, besieged by three knights wearing the blue-and-gold colours of Toulouse. A path opened through the mêlée of slashing weapons, but still Reynaud hesitated.

Leonor pivoted and flew past him towards the staircase. Heart pounding in her throat, she measured the distance to safety. Ten more steps. Five. The sound of Reynaud's laboured breathing at her back told her he was following.

She reached the first step, but a hoarse cry stopped her in her tracks. She whirled to see Baudoin de Beziers crumple to the floor. Without thinking, she brushed past Reynaud and ran towards the knight's motionless form.

Benjamin shielded her from the crowd of angry knights with his own lanky body. 'Run!' he shouted in her ear. He pushed her towards the stairs. 'Save yourself.'

With a last look at de Beziers's lifeless body, she caught up her gown in one hand and raced towards the staircase and Reynaud.

In the dark bailey, two saddled horses stamped impatiently. Hurriedly Reynaud mounted his grey destrier, then bent to lift her up and settled her in front of him. He grabbed the lead of her palfrey and dug his heels into his own mount.

Raucous shouts rose behind the inner gate, and both animals jolted forwards, clattered across the drawbridge and over the cobbled yard towards the north fortress gate.

Why the north gate? she wondered. Surely they must head west, towards Moyanne? Before she could voice the question, Reynaud spoke at her temple.

'They will not think to come this direction, towards Toulouse, since I am known there. And unwelcome.'

She nodded. Then they were through the gate in a thunder of hooves and out into the enveloping black night. Behind them another horse thundered over the planks, then veered off in the opposite direction. Reynaud chuckled deep in his throat.

Safe.

Or perhaps not safe, since they now rode towards Toulouse.

'I know of a place,' Reynaud said as if reading her mind. 'A Cathar fortress hidden in the mountains.'

Brother Pierre—no, *Bishop* Pierre—had slipped into his hand the gate key to the abandoned Cathar refuge. One of God's miracles.

He cradled Leonor against his chest. They were out of danger for the moment, thanks to the foresight of Baudoin de Beziers, who had known of the grudge the knights of Toulouse bore him. Before supper, the gallant older knight had 'misplaced' the saddles of all the knights of Toulouse.

His wounded shoulder throbbed, and blood oozed from his chest where de Rodez's sword had sliced through his tunic.

He sucked in a full, deep breath of the scented night air and pulled Leonor's body tight against his. Closing his eyes, he weighed his Templar vows against his love for the woman he now held in his arms.

He had nothing to offer but himself, bastard-born and landless.

So be it. If he had nothing else in this life—not father, nor lands, nor surname to call his own—one night with Leonor would be enough to last him all his days. He would ask for nothing more as long as he lived.

Chapter Twenty-Six

Montèguy fortress rose like a mirage before Leonor's eyes. Clinging precariously to the side of a rocky mountain, the grey-black walls cascaded down the sheer granite cliff like a waterfall of stone.

The horses clopped their way up and up the narrow, twisting path to the massive gate of age-blackened iron. No light shone. Nothing moved within or without the huge, silent structure. The place looked as if it were enchanted.

Reynaud drew the destrier to a halt and sat motionless, listening. The moon had long since set, and in the darkness small night animals rustled under the pine trees that softened the bare face of the mountainside. He gave a low whistle. After a moment, a nightingale began to sing and she heard him exhale in relief. The castle was deserted.

Laying the destrier's reins in her hands, he dismounted, favouring his wounded shoulder. They had stopped some leagues back to bathe and dress his wounds, but even so the gash still throbbed.

He fit the odd-shaped metal key into the gate lock and, using both hands, twisted it to the right. The gate creaked open on long-rusted hinges.

Relief surged through Leonor's tense body, followed by something else, a sweet, mysterious sense of extraordinary well-being. What could be wrong with her? She had watched a man die this very night, yet at this moment she felt naught but pure joy.

It was not only their escape, and the safety it brought. It was being with Reynaud, feeling his hard man's body pressed at her back these long hours on horseback, aware of his every move, his every breath.

He reached up, encircled her waist, and lifted her down. With an odd sound in his throat, he set her before him; then for a long moment stood quite still, as if struggling with something.

Leonor's pulse quickened. In his eyes she saw heat and longing. He wanted her. A flame licked at her heart, her skin, and a hot, sweet thread of desire laced deep into her body. She held her breath.

'Ah,' he breathed at last. 'Life is a joyless dance without love. Death comes to all in the end, but I do not wish to leave this life without knowing your love this one night.'

'I think…' She searched for the right words to speak what lay in her heart. 'I think that love is not exclusive, my Reynaud. One can love both God and His church. And,' she added softly, 'a woman. Why else would God make you a man first, and a holy knight second?'

'It is you I love, Lea. Not the Church or the Templars.'

'Nay,' she said, her voice gentle. 'I believe it is all one—the turning earth, the sky that changes from dark to light, a man, a woman. It is all the same. God made it all in His image. And,' she added, 'He is guiding us when we follow our hearts.'

'You speak like a Cathar,' he said, a hint of laughter in his voice. He closed his arms around her.

'I speak like a woman full-blown,' she murmured. She looked up into his strained face. 'One who loves you.'

She felt his body tremble.

'Though my vows forbid it, I would have you, Leonor.'

She stirred in his arms, pressed the tips of her aching breasts against his chest. 'Take me, then. We know not what the morrow may bring. Yet whatever it is to be, I will face it gladly if we can be together this night.'

He sucked in his breath and without a word took her hand and pushed through the castle gate. 'One night will scarce be long enough for what I want of you.'

The bed dominated the tiny chamber. Covered in red damask, powdery with dried lavender, the huge curtained four-poster faced the narrow third-floor window and the small stone fireplace on the adjacent wall. How Reynaud found his way up that twisting staircase in the dark she could not fathom. He had been here before, she supposed. He seemed to know this fortress.

A silvery light poured through the single paned window as Reynaud flipped the cover off the bed. Underneath were fresh linen sheets, neatly turned down. The scent of rosemary and dried lavender permeated the room.

His hand touched her shoulder. 'Do not move,' he murmured. 'I would unlace your gown.'

Her heart leaped at the touch of his fingers at her neck. The day's heat had ebbed to a velvety softness, leaving the late summer air thick and smelling of wild roses. She raised her arms, felt his hands move back and forth over her body as he loosened her outer robe and smoothed it down over her hips.

Warm, scented air wafted over her bare shoulders. Reynaud laid one finger at the base of her throat and her body throbbed to life. He stroked upwards to her chin, then slowly drew his hand down to the neckline of her chemise.

Her breath stopped. He leaned down, traced the path of his hand with his tongue, moving langorously up to her neck, along her jawbone to the shell of her ear. He circled his warm wet tongue around the sensitive edge, then gently dipped into the inner recess.

A jolt of sensation pierced below her belly, and she gasped aloud with pleasure. His quick breath told her it pleasured him, as well.

She told herself not to move, to let him proceed as he wished. His touch was like exquisite fire on her skin. She felt her skin swell and flush, felt her body fill with hot light. *Please, God, let me remember every moment of this.*

He lifted his good arm to her shoulder, unknotted the ribbon at her bosom and slowly pushed the light muslin down. He smoothed his warm palms up her bare arms and over her shoulders. Deliberately he brought his mouth to her other ear, probing again with his tongue.

Her belly contracted. Below, the sweet ache blossomed between her thighs, and she moaned.

Breathing softly into her ear, Reynaud moved his hands to her breasts. Beneath his fingers her nipples hardened, ached. Ah, what ecstasy, to be touched so by a man.

He circled his hands over her breasts, then slid them slowly down her ribcage to her waist, taking the loosened chemise down as well. He stroked her buttocks, caressing them, cupping them with his splayed fingers.

In spite of herself, Leonor began to move. She raised first one arm, then the other, over her head, arching her back to thrust her breasts forwards, longing for him to touch them again.

A low chuckle of satisfaction rumbled deep in his throat. Still gently kneading her bottom, he bent and circled his tongue about one swollen nipple, over it, around it, again and yet again.

Her breathing grew shallow and ragged. She could die of pleasure at this very moment! Oh, she wanted so much of him.

His hand moved to her inner thigh, stroking up and down, purposefully coming closer and closer to the soft triangle of dark hair between her legs. And then he took her other nipple in his mouth. His hot, wet tongue circled and sucked, and at the same time he gently parted her legs and slid one finger inside her swollen outer lips.

'Reynaud,' she murmured. *'Reynaud.'* She wanted him to move his hand, touch her, stroke her.

But he did not.

Instead, he began to suck lightly on her nipple. And he began to talk to her, his voice low and urgent. Throaty, inarticulate phrases punctuated his uneven breathing. She could not follow his words, save for recognizing her name spoken over and over. Leonor. Leonor, *ya jamiilah*. He said it again, his voice hoarse, trembling.

Joy lifted her, transported her spirit. Her mouth opened, her tongue emerged to slowly wet her lips. She felt real and unreal at the same time, more herself than she had ever been before, yet at the same time aware of new strengths and mysteries, depths she had not known she possessed.

Holy Mary, look down on this woman, your servant, and bless her joy. For surely such pleasure is unlike any other on earth. And just as surely, God Himself intended it to be so.

She twined her fingers into Reynaud's dark hair, tipped her head towards the ceiling and smiled. No happiness would ever equal this.

He lifted his head, sought her mouth. At the same

time he began circling his finger slowly back and forth over the exquisitely sensitive spot above her opening.

With his tongue, he grazed her mouth, teasing her lips until she groaned aloud with wanting. He laughed softly into her open mouth, then again uttered her name. Leonor. *Ya jamiilah.* He dipped his tongue past her teeth and again slid his finger inside her.

She gasped. Panting for breath, she moved against him, instinctively seeking deeper penetration. His warm breath swirled into her mouth. She moaned, cried his name. She would die of ecstasy before this was done. Still, she knew he prolonged each movement, each touch to draw her pleasure out as long as possible. She wished it never to end.

'Reynaud,' she sighed under his hot mouth. *'Reynaud.'*

Her hands found their way under his tunic to his bare chest. She pulled the torn silk garment up, skimmed her fingers over his hard, smooth torso, avoiding the sword cut near his breastbone. She caressed the taut muscles of his back, then swept two fingers lightly back and forth over his nipples.

He groaned with pleasure. On impulse, she lowered her mouth and swirled the tip of her tongue around each brown nub. He stiffened for an instant, and she heard his breath hiss sharply in. The sound was intensely satisfying. His heartbeat hammered under her lips, his irregular breath rasped in and out.

There was more to this than lips and tongues and

hands. The physical touching was just the beginning. She drank in the feeling of power, of connec-
tion with another human spirit.

Her heart sang as her body opened to him. Her
fingers touched the lacings of his chausses, and with
a quick tug she pulled the knot free.

His undergarment fell away, and his engorged
manhood pressed against her thighs. He slipped one
hand under her bottom and lifted her. The tip of his
erect shaft moved over her mound, slid slowly, inex-
orably forwards until it spread the outer flower of her
woman's centre and brushed delicately back and
forth against the hot, moist tissue. He bent his head,
seeking her mouth. She opened her lips under his,
felt him tremble.

Without a word he moved them to the bed,
pressed her down on the sheet and spread her thighs
wide. 'It will not be easy,' he murmured. 'It is your
first time.'

'And the last time,' she reminded in a soft
whisper. 'I do not want it to be easy. I want to
remember it for ever.'

His mouth moved over her skin like hot silk, over
her breasts, down her belly. And then, very, very
slowly he thrust his tongue through the fine dark
hair curling between her thighs, parting her petalled
lips, probing in lazy circles. When the warm tip of
his tongue entered her, she cried out, 'Yes, Rey. *Yes!*'

He withdrew, washing a soft stream of cooling
air over her as he exhaled against her slick, wet
centre. She writhed and moaned as he spread her,

tasted her. She felt something stretch within her spirit, stretch and break and mend itself, stronger than before.

I am ready for him. She reached to him, raised him to face her.

Reynaud moved his body over hers, straddling her, and looked down into her face. Holding her eyes, he lowered himself, thrust slowly in, then out, once, twice more, each time probing deeper.

Leonor arched to take him, raised both arms over her head, moaning his name. She cried out once as he plunged deep inside her, then began to move with him. Breath for breath, thrust for thrust, she matched him. Bathed in perspiration, her breath coming now in quick, shallow gasps, she exulted in the sheer animal beauty of coupling. As if from a great distance she heard his voice calling her name, and she sobbed aloud.

A shuddering spasm convulsed her body, and she screamed. Her inner muscles contracted, pulsing in slow waves of ecstasy as her mind soared into a black velvety space.

Reynaud watched her face, watched her darkened eyes close, her mouth contort as she convulsed under him. He thrust hard once more and felt his seed begin to spurt. Ah, his body was breaking into flame.

With a shout, he plunged deep and let the spasms wash over him until he was completely spent.

God speaks slowly, he thought in wonder. *But exceedingly clear.* The threads of his life, so long unravelled, were at last weaving themselves into a pattern.

With this one woman, this one act, he had found some part of himself he had searched for all his life.

He buried himself in her, wrapped both arms around her naked body and wept.

Chapter Twenty-Seven

Leonor awoke with a start. Something was amiss. The sheets beside her where Reynaud's body had lain were still warm, but he was gone. Gone, too, were his tunic and chausses.

His leather boots still lay in the corner where he had kicked them last night. Her thighs ached at the memory. How wanton she was! She could not get enough of him.

The chamber door banged open, and Reynaud appeared, his dark curls tousled, a half-opened parcel of brown bread and cheese in one hand. 'I found it in my saddlebag, wrapped in oiled paper, along with your riding trousers and a clean tunic. Count Roger's wife must have seen to it.'

Dear Lord, bless Jannet for thinking of practical matters amidst the turmoil. She bit into the cheese. 'Oh, how delicious! I am so hungry this morning, and everything tastes so—'

Reynaud's laughter rang, and she broke off. Her face grew warm, then cold, then warm again. He knew! And he felt the same, she could see it in his eyes, heating to emerald fire as he watched her gobble the cheese.

'Rey, could we…?'

'Nay, we cannot. There is not time enough. We must reach Moyanne as soon as we can. I myself must tell Count Henri of his son's death. Get you dressed, *jamiilah*. We have many leagues before us.'

They rode hard for three days, a grueling journey except for the soft, heated nights when they clung to each other in desperate hunger and joy. Reynaud drove the horses as never before, whether to cover as much ground as possible or to make camp and bed down with her, she neither knew nor cared. They were drunk with each other. For two nights she tasted little that mattered save for the salty-sweet flavour of his skin.

Now, they drew their weary horses up in the shade of the ancient spreading oak at the bend of the River Oloron. This would be their last night together. She sat motionless and a crippling sense of loss washed over her.

It must end. She knew it, saw it in his face when he kissed her, held her close. He was a Templar, a warrior monk, with no name or rank save what he earned by his skill at arms and his missions for his Grand Master. And she was daughter to the Vizier of Granada.

Tomorrow they would ride through the gate of Moyanne as cousins, not as lovers. And then he would ride away from her to take up the duties of his order. Her heart and soul would go with him.

If this was what it meant to love a man, small wonder that women died of broken hearts.

Reynaud's hands closed about her waist, lifted her off her mare and set her before him. His lips brushed against her temple and she closed her eyes and forgot all else.

Gently he pulled her tunic over her head, then tugged loose the knot of her trouser cord. The silky material dropped about her ankles and she stepped out of the garment, kicking off her worn leather slippers as she did so.

Reynaud grasped her bare leg, lifting it until her knee brushed his upper thigh. Instantly his breath caught. His chausses bulged with his engorged manhood.

He stepped quickly away from her, towards the river bank, shedding his garments as he walked. His sweat-covered torso glistened in the mauve-and-peach light of the dying sun. Without a backwards glance, he dove into the river.

At his silent invitation, she moved to the river's edge, waded into the cool, blue-green water and swam towards him with languid strokes. He stood up in the chest-deep water and her breasts brushed against his hard-muscled chest. He slid one hand beneath her bottom and pulled her close.

Incredibly, she felt him enter her. He moved

inside her and her nipples swelled into hard, aching buds.

Reynaud laughed with delight, his voice young and carefree. Dipping his head, he licked the base of her throat, then her breasts, with his warm tongue, all the while gently moving inside her. She grasped his head, twined her fingers into his dark hair and held him close.

His lips moved over hers as he thrust inside her, lifting her hips with both hands to let his member probe deep. Slowly, deliberately, he worked her body back and forth, his hands at her back. She felt the hot tension coil and build, driving her towards release.

Abruptly he scooped her up and waded out of the river. He laid her on a bed of matted thyme, then knelt beside her. The pungent scent of the herb filled her nostrils. Impulsively she reached out and broke off a tiny frond, crushed it against her body, between her breasts, over her belly. It seemed an odd gesture in a way, but when she felt Reynaud's warm, wet tongue between her breasts, then at the small of her back, she knew it was not odd. Nothing was odd when it came to his loving; he was skilled beyond her understanding. She would remember the scent of thyme for the rest of her days.

He waited, leaving her poised on the brink of entry but under her own control, and she smiled. He held himself back so she could follow her own needs, could learn about herself.

And so she would. She lowered her mouth to his, traced his lips with the tip of her tongue, revelling in his quick intake of air. At the same time, she tipped her hips, caught his hard phallus against the delicate inner lips of her centre and eased the smooth tip just inside her. Very slowly, she rotated her hips. His hands convulsively kneaded her buttocks.

She longed to tease him. At the same time, she wanted to possess him. Her body had a life of its own, as did her spirit. She understood now. The love act could meld these two separate parts into a whole.

The thought fed her passion in a way she had not expected. A fierce need for penetration built in her, but at the same time she knew that the longer she withheld her own pleasure, the greater would be their mutual rapture, the sense of oneness, at the moment of culmination.

His warm breath gusted past her ear. She lifted her head, held his eyes in a long, steady look and smiled. She would take her time.

His brows lifted in a question, then his mouth quirked into a grin. She leaned back against his bent knees and felt his shaft sink deep inside her. Closing her eyes at the delicious sensation, she rocked forwards until her nipples grazed his chest.

She loosened her hair and spread the dark, silky curtain over his face and chest. Listening to his heart pound, she matched his breathing, matched the rhythm of his hands circling over her breasts with the measured thrusting of her hips. His rigid member filled her, slid in and out of her slick, wet entrance as she stretched and twisted above him.

She edged towards her release, and sharp, savage joy pierced her. Panting, she worked to bring

Reynaud with her, taking him more slowly, more deeply than before. Flame licked her, and she exploded. Reynaud clasped her close, his own climax jerking his body in uncontrollable shudders.

Oh! Loving was fierce and honest, the body breaking into flower on a rack of fire.

But she knew there would be a price.

Count Henri rose and grasped Reynaud's hand, his face alight. 'Welcome, my boy, welcome! We have missed you these few weeks. And how I have missed the sound of Leonor's harp.'

Reynaud hesitated. 'She did not bring her harp with her.'

The count's bushy eyebrows rose. 'Not brought— But why?'

The older man's keen blue eyes studied Reynaud, took in his dusty, travel-stained tunic. 'Ah, I see. You travelled quickly.'

'My lord, I bring sad news. I—' He took a step towards the thin, proud man. He must speak now, before someone else arrived from Carcassonne with tales of Bernard de Rodez's death.

The count eyed him calmly, his gaze unflinching. 'Speak, then.'

Gently Reynaud urged the older man to resume his seat. Then he knelt before him, looked directly into the lined face, and lifted the old man's shaking hands in both of his. 'I would to God I could spare you this, Henri, but I cannot. Your son, Bernard de Rodez, is dead.'

The count's mild blue eyes glazed. His mouth twisted, but no sound escaped his lips. At last he drew a wheezy breath.

'How? In the tourney? I knew of the tourney, of course,' he said with a weary sigh. 'Ever does my brother Roger relish his tourneys.'

Reynaud's heart stuttered. 'It was not in the tourney. I fought him, it is true, but in hand-to-hand combat to save Leonor.'

'Leonor?' The blood drained from Henri's cheeks. 'What mischief had Bernard wrought this time?'

Reynaud hesitated. 'He accosted Leonor. Swords were drawn. I—I had to strike, lest he harm her.'

The count nodded, listening.

'De Rodez had slandered her. I fought to clear her of the charge. I am sorry, Henri. It was I who killed him.' There was no need to tell the old man more.

For some time the Count did not speak. Then, his voice distant, he said, 'In a way I am not surprised. The boy was a strange one from the first moment he drew breath. But he was my only son. Heir to my name and all that I hold.'

'Henri,' Reynaud murmured. 'I wish I had not done it.' He resisted the impulse to pull the trembling man into his arms.

The count swallowed hard. 'Tell me the rest.'

'Your brother, Count Roger, helped us escape.' Reynaud bowed his head before the count. 'I wanted to tell you of the deed myself, knowing how it would pain you.'

Count Henri withdrew one hand from Reynaud's

grasp. Reaching out, he ruffled Reynaud's hair. 'Grieve not, man,' he said, his voice shaking. 'I knew long ago my son would not live to old age. He was…rash. Greedy. Someone would have killed him, sooner or later. I am sorry it had to be you.'

Reynaud blinked back tears at the resignation in the older man's voice. His chest ached with remorse and with something else, as well. The gentle pressure of the count's hand on his head touched him deeply. How he had longed for such a gesture when he was a boy. His foster father, Hakim, had been harsh in parenting. Only his uncle, Hassam, had ever shown approval of him.

His chest constricted. While he was here at Moyanne, awaiting new orders from his Templar Grand Master, he would ease Count Henri's burden as best he could. And then…

He closed his eyes for a brief moment. Then, God willing, he must take his leave of Leonor and resume his life as a knight of the Temple.

The count rose and laid one veined hand on Reynaud's shoulder. 'Alais and I will expect you at supper tonight. From the look of you, we could both use some strong Gascony wine, could we not?'

Three hours later, Reynaud smiled down into his cup of unwatered wine, listening for the third time in as many hours to the count's wife, Alais, sing the praises of her wolfhound's litter of pups. The woman seemed besotted with the bitch's offspring. One would think she, and not the hound, was the mother.

'Alais hungers still for young ones,' Count Henri murmured at his elbow. 'Even more, now that my son…'

He left the thought unfinished. Reynaud's heart wrenched at the far-away look in the older man's eyes. He drained his cup and signalled the wine bearer.

'Thank you, my boy. Thank you,' the count breathed. 'I rarely imbibe so late of an evening, but tonight it seems…needful.'

Reynaud touched his pewter cup to the count's jewel-studded goblet. 'I will join you, then.' Anything to take his mind off Leonor, seated only tantalising inches away from him at the high table. She picked at her food without uttering a word, listening to Lady Alais talk of weaning her pups.

Her presence, the elusive spicy fragrance of her hair, the memory of her soft warmth beside him made him ache with wanting. He would not be with her this night, would not take her in the sweet, heated silence of loving. She would lie alone in her chamber and he—

He would pace the castle ramparts until dawn.

Count Henri leaned towards him. 'Drink up, man. It heals the soul.'

Reynaud gave a short laugh. Does it, indeed? He could dull his body's craving with wine, but it would not ease the emptiness inside him. The thought of life without Leonor made everything seem grey and drab.

Perhaps Henri was right. He would have more

wine. A great deal more wine. At least he could keep the count company.

Henri's filmy blue eyes followed his wife's progress as she circled the room with the dancers. 'Alais is a good wife,' he confided, his voice low. 'Always has been.'

Reynaud murmured an assent. He could not keep his eyes off Leonor, dressed in pale yellow silk, her hair bound up with gold cord and covered with a gauzy veil. Her smile made the hunger in his heart unbearable.

What they had known these past few days was all they would ever have. Eventually she would marry. He clenched his jaw at the thought of his Leonor in another man's arms. Dragging his gaze away, he focused instead on tiny, plump Lady Alais, moving with the circle of dancers.

'Women,' the count mused. 'So different, yet so much the same under the skin.'

Reynaud grunted.

'I never did come to love Bernard's mother,' Henri continued, in an undertone. 'I thought I would in time, but it was not to be. I missed her, though, when the fever took her. And,' he added in a tone well covered by the sound of rebec and pipe, 'that spring, when I travelled from Navarre to Aragon to visit Leonor's grandfather, I fell in love for the first time.'

Reynaud shifted in his seat. He did not want to talk of love—the count's or anyone else's. Not when Leonor was so near and yet so far from him in possibility that he could not trust himself even to touch her hand. He managed a nod, then drained his wine cup.

'From the beginning it was not an appropriate match,' Henry sighed. 'I was much older, and still in mourning for my wife, and she was but a serving maid. Yet the girl loved me, I think. She comforted me much that spring, put my loneliness to flight as only a woman can. She was a virgin when I took her,' he confided in a whisper. 'Ah, what a golden time it was.'

Reynaud tipped his chair back. 'You were fortunate.' His voice shook.

'I was,' the count acknowledged. 'Were it not for my heritage, I would have married her. But, as it was, I bore the obligations of my station and wed another.' He tipped his head towards Alais, now leading the circle of women in a spirited dance.

'But I never forgot that sweet maid, nor all the times of our loving when she came to me.'

'Do you think of her still?' Reynaud inquired in a gentle voice.

'Aye, still.' The old count exhaled in a long sigh. 'Have you never loved a woman?'

Reynaud's gut clenched. He took a deep breath and met Count Henri's steady gaze. 'I am bastard born, my lord. And a Templar. I have not the right to love a woman.'

'*Eh bien.* How was it you were raised by an Arab family in Granada?'

'My foster-aunt brought me newborn to the house of Hakim in a reed basket. I was raised by foster-parents—Leonor's Arab uncle.'

Count Henri stared at him. With an effort he brought his lips together. 'Such marriages are rare, but not unknown. Ah, then you are not half-Arab, as I had thought.'

Reynaud pressed the older man's hand. 'I am not. Would to God I knew my heritage, but I do not.' He rose and strode from the hall.

Alone on the parapet wall, he sucked in great gulps of the soft night air and struggled to sort out his own thoughts. He liked Count Henri, admired the gentle authority with which he administered his demesne, even envied him his wife, the Lady Alais. Were he to choose a man to revere other than his Uncle Hassam, he could choose none better than Henri, Count of Moyanne.

But one could not choose one's father. Pain lanced his chest. He had never fit anywhere, was always on the outside. Heritage, lineage were all a man had in this life, save for exploits in battle, feats of arms that gained fame and perhaps some fortune.

But now he knew that such things alone were not enough. Worldly success did not define a man's worth. He gripped the rough stone ledge until his knuckles ached and turned his face up to the sky where a blush of peach foretold another dawn. Something inside him started to crumble.

Chapter Twenty-Eight

Leonor jolted from an exhausted sleep and dragged her heavy limbs from the narrow bed to peer out the casement. In the courtyard below hooves clattered and men shouted. *What now?*

The coppery sun beat down on a courtyard milling with people. Travellers, by the look of them. A knight and his lady, accompanied by a cowled monk and one—no, two clerics. Plus an entire retinue of knights and men-at-arms. She noted with relief that all wore the scarlet-and-black colours of Carcassonne, not the blue and gold of Toulouse. Count Roger and Jannet... It had to be!

And there, just emerging through the inner gate, a tall figure in dark robes, riding a mule.

Benjamin! Hurriedly she pulled on her chemise, donned the first gown she laid her hand on and flew down the stone stairway in her bare feet.

'Benjamin!'

'Leonora, *regalada*!' The old man slipped from the mule and clasped her close. 'Thank God you are safe. I died a thousand deaths each day when we found no trace of you and Reynaud. But then no doubt you followed an untravelled road?'

'We did,' she murmured. How 'untravelled' her old tutor would never know, though by the soft look in his black eyes he had guessed.

'*Kerida,*' Benjamin said after a long look into her face. 'I am a tired man. I would sell my soul for a bath and a pallet near the kitchen.'

Sell my soul... She had not yet sought out the priest to confess her sins of the past four days!

Strange, but she felt not the least bit sinful. No matter what the teaching of Holy Writ, learned by heart before she could read, she could not feel there was sin in loving Reynaud, nor in coupling with him.

Reynaud did not appear until supper. He seated himself next to her, but said nothing.

'You missed the mass spoken for Henri's son,' she observed, taking care that the clank of knives and platters covered her words.

'I did not sleep last night,' he replied. 'I rode into the woods to…think.' She watched his fingers clench and unclench around the handle of his eating knife. So fine and slim they were. Lover's hands.

Her breath caught. 'I, too, slept little,' she whispered. 'It is difficult without you.'

His shoulders stiffened. 'Not merely difficult, Lea. It is agony.'

After that, they gave up any show of making conversation. It was enough at this moment to feel his warmth beside her.

Or almost enough. She longed to curl herself against his hard muscled chest and share the day's events. Her skin burned with wanting him, but she dared not even touch his hand.

Think of other things!

'That monk,' she began after Reynaud replenished her wine cup. 'The strange one who rode from Carcassonne with Benjamin?'

Reynaud sipped from his cup, his eyes resting on hers. 'Monk?'

'That one.' She gestured down the table with her knife. 'Near the end.'

His gaze travelled from face to face along the length of the table. When his pupils widened, Leonor knew he had found the man.

'No monk that,' he muttered.

She stared at him. 'He spoke the mass today for Henri's son. Surely he is not an imposter?'

Reynaud's lips compressed into a thin smile. 'Not in the way you think, but an imposter none the less. More than that I cannot say, even to you.'

'But—'

'There is a reason why such a one comes in disguise, Lea. Chances are I will know of it before the night ends.'

He returned his gaze to the platter of roast venison before them and with a decisive motion pierced a slice of the meat with his knife. 'Only one thing am

I certain of,' he murmured as he cut the meat into two portions and lifted one on to her plate.

An icy hand clenched her stomach. 'And that is?'

'This time, you will not come with me.'

She kept her voice steady. 'That I know, Rey.'

'And another thing I am certain of,' he breathed. He turned his head towards her and held her gaze. 'I love you,' he whispered. 'Only you.'

Her heart caught. 'That also do I know.'

She touched his hand, then knotted her fingers in her lap to keep from touching him again. Reynaud laid one warm palm over her balled fist and squeezed hard. 'Drink some wine, Lea. It is unwatered, as is mine. It dulls the edge of wanting.'

She nodded and reached for her wine cup, her lids stinging.

The monk's penetrating brown eyes met Reynaud's. Purposefully the man inclined his head and fingered the metal cross at his breast, and a jolt of unease stabbed below Reynaud's heart. When was a call to duty so subtly given?

Count Henri rose to introduce Brother Pierre, and then he knew his remaining time in Moyanne was short.

He dropped his gaze before the prelate's intent look and reached for Leonor's hand, still fisted in her lap. Not yet would he leave her. He would savour these last moments as long as he could. He would have the rest of his life to remember them.

God's eyes, he was weary in spirit, torn between

duty to the Templars and his love for Leonor. His chest ached. His head pounded with each beat of his heart. But his soul ached most of all, and it ached for Leonor.

The monk rose and advanced towards the dais, drew back his cowl and turned his pale, angular face on the assembled company.

'It is not "Brother" Pierre, my lord Henri, but Bishop Pierre, of Chalons. I am spokesman for Pope Alexander in Rome, and I come on a matter of some urgency.' He lifted one veined hand. 'If I may speak?'

'Speak, speak,' echoed through the hall. Count Henri waved him forwards, and the bishop stepped to the dais and turned to face the hushed hall. His sharp eyes scanned the crowd, waiting until the silence hammered against the stone walls, then he lifted his paper-thin voice.

'The Holy Church calls for a new crusade against the infidel. A Frankish crusade.' He let the murmurs die away before he continued. With every word, his voice grew more strident.

'Each passing day the threat of conquest and death draws ever closer to your doorstep. We must attack the foes of Christ and His Holy Church, must wrest the Christian lands from the Saracen without delay.'

Reynaud went rigid. He saw what the old fox was up to. Louis of France and the Christian kings of Aragon and Castile wanted to attack not Jerusalem, but Spain. It was not a crusade to free a holy city, but military aggression to gain lands. A war to drive out the Arabs who had dominated Al-Andalus for five hundred years. This was simply papal chicanery.

Reynaud's belly roiled. In the next instant he found himself on his feet. 'It is to Jerusalem that Christian warriors should journey, not to Spain. The Saracen threat is a tale carried by troubadours. They struggle among themselves to hold on to what they have, and trouble us not.'

Bishop Pierre turned expressionless eyes on him. 'Ah, Reynaud. I wondered when we should meet again. I bear a message for you. From your Grand Master, Bertrand de Blanquefort.'

Reynaud murmured a silent prayer. He could guess the content.

He cleared his throat. 'My lord bishop, it is well known that Aragon holds lands in Gascony and Navarre. Would Louis of France march against his brother Christians in search of conquest?'

The bishop's sharp eyes hardened. 'It is principle, not land, that is in question here.'

'What principle, my lord?' Reynaud challenged.

The prelate jerked. 'Lands in a Christian kingdom cannot be held by unbelievers. Infidels.'

'The Saracens are not "unbelievers",' Reynaud said quietly. 'They simply follow their own holy book, which is different from ours. To the Arabs, *we* are the infidel.'

The bishop's voice hardened. 'You have been too long in the Holy Land, Templar. You see things from too many sides.'

'Aye,' Reynaud agreed, his voice flat. 'That I do.

So should we all, if we follow God's word. Does He not say that all men are broth—?'

'Enough!'

The word cut into him like the tolling of a church bell. At once his life was clear, transparent as a gauze veil. His gorge rose at the thought of more killing.

But he was a warrior, was he not? He killed where and when he was ordered.

No more, he resolved. Never again could he stomach the ravages of battle, the sight of mangled bodies left to rot, unshriven, behind fortress walls.

'Reynaud,' Bishop Pierre thundered, 'you will obey Holy Church in this, else you will never know God's glory.'

'I know already God's glory,' he said steadily. He pressed his hand over his chest. 'It is here, in my heart. I do not need to kill a man to win God's favour.'

'That is blasphemy!' the bishop shouted.

'I do not think so. I think it is truth.' He had already been given God's grace. Leonor's love was a precious gift; it had illuminated his path to himself.

Across the hall, Count Henri's gaze met his. Very slowly the older man raised his hand in an eloquent gesture. The chair scraped as the count rose to his feet.

'Answer the call of God, Reynaud. Accept the challenge God offers you.'

Reynaud's spine froze.

Quiet descended like a pall of grey fog. Then a clamour of surprised voices erupted. Reynaud bent over Leonor's upturned face and spoke in her ear. 'I am called once more.'

Her grey eyes widened. 'Rey?' she whispered.

He spoke rapidly, his voice low. 'But it does not matter. I have given up everything to find myself, even my Templar vows. I now know the man I have become, and I must stand for what I believe.'

An invisible net dropped over him. Was he but a pawn of conflicting forces?

A month ago he was first a Templar, a servant of God, and a warrior. Now he was a man unto himself. Bishop Pierre would never understand this. He was only half-sure he himself understood the change in his heart.

But it was enough. Something inside him had drawn a battle line, and beyond it he could not, would not, force himself to step.

His gut clenched. God help him, never in his life had he felt so alone.

He swallowed over a throat so tight it ached. God would not pity him for what his integrity had cost him. God would expect him to re-order his life.

Chapter Twenty-Nine

Benjamin watched Leonor's slender figure move away from Reynaud and the priest who harangued him and mount the stairs at the far end of the room, her back straight, her dark head held high. His lamb. His precious lamb. He brushed his sleeve across his damp eyelids. She would stiffen her spine and go on with her life in spite of Reynaud's call to duty. In spite of her heartbreak.

She would winter with her great-aunt in Navarre, and with those two scapegrace minstrels who had followed her from Carcassonne. Even an old fool could see she would make her mark in the world as a troubadour.

From his sleeve he drew an embroidered linen handerchief, a gift from the baker's widow in Carcassonne, and noisily blew his nose into it. How he would miss her!

He snuffled into the scrap of linen. Aye, it hurt to love someone.

* * *

Reynaud stared at the two unsmiling men seated before him in Count Henri's solar and clenched his hands at his sides. Bishop Pierre of Chalons and Count Henri surveyed him with hard, expressionless eyes. What more could he say to the prelate and the count? He would not obey his Grand Master's orders. No true Templar knight behaved in such a way.

But no matter the cost, he would speak the truth.

The count gestured to his left. 'Sit you down, man. You look half-dead.'

Reynaud studied Henri's carefully masked expression. 'I will stand.'

Bishop Pierre snorted. 'I'll wager he will sit before this is over, Henri. Do not urge him further.'

Reynaud's belly lurched. Before *what* was over? Would he be exiled from Navarre? Driven away or…he flinched inwardly…forced into a monastery to atone for his sin in breaking his Templar vows?

Ah, that was it, then. He would not be forced out of the order, merely retired in dishonour to life as a cleric. A celibate cleric. He would sooner die.

'Reynaud.' Bishop Pierre's voice was so penetrating Count Henri visibly jerked. 'I wonder if one such as yourself is suited to what we have in mind?'

'"We", my lord? Who is "we"?'

The prelate sent him a long look. 'Those you see before you, your bishop, and your host, Count Henri. And in addition your Grand Master, Bertrand de Blanquefort, and Pope Alexander, of course. Aragon's king…and perhaps Louis of France, as well.'

His heart constricted. He had served them to the best of his ability, both on the dusty field of battle and in spacious audience chambers that smelled of incense and spices instead of sweat and horse dung. It was a harsh justice that punished a man for one mistake after a lifetime of loyal service.

He faced his accusers. 'I am ready to hear sentence.'

Bishop Pierre rose and stepped towards him. 'Then, Reynaud, listen closely. It is to our advantage that negotiation and treaty replace the spilling of blood in the matter of lands held by the Arabs. You are experienced in diplomatic missions. You speak the language of the Saracen. You are skilled with both sword and word. By way of your past efforts, you are known and respected by both Arab and Christian. And,' the bishop grated, 'you owe the Templars a favour. A penance, shall we say?'

Had he heard aright? They were not going to banish him to a monastery? Because… He drew in a careful breath. They *needed* him?

He bit back the chuckle that rose in his throat. Penance be damned. They were desperate men. They needed a diplomatic envoy. Only the fear of finding one's back to the wall brought such an offer. He almost laughed out loud.

'What would you give that I do this?' He held his breath, afraid to move even one eyelash.

'What do you ask?' Bishop Pierre asked quietly.

Reynaud was silent so long Count Henri shifted in his chair and gave a surreptitious tug at the bishop's habit. Reynaud waited another full minute before replying.

'I would be honourably released from my Templar vows.'

'Granted,' the prelate said instantly. 'And?'

And? He hesitated, his heart beginning to hammer against his chest wall. Did he dare ask for what he wanted most?

Bishop Pierre studied him at length, his dark eyes expressionless.

He opened his lips and formed the words. 'I wish to marry the Lady Leonor.'

From her open window, Leonor waved farewell to Benjamin's black-robed figure until her vision misted and she could no longer see. Her old tutor was returning to Granada.

She laid her head on the casement sill and wept. What had she now, save the empty shell of a life? A tormented body she could not give to the man she loved, and a gift for music when she no longer cared to sing?

She raised her head, brushed her hand across her eyes. How far away the place of her birth was now. How long ago it was when she had been young and untried, her heart untouched.

She did not want to return to Granada; better to stay here in Moyanne and go forwards with what life she had left. She would learn the songs sung by Brian of Orkney and Andreas, and she would make her way as she had once dreamed, as a troubadour. Thus would she heal the wound in her heart.

She would never again feel whole, as she did when she was with Reynaud. Her songs might express more depth now, more understanding than before the stretching and unfolding of her innermost being. But ah, God, the cost.

Was this the price of loving a man? Truly, it was no easy task to be a woman. At the moment she had not even the stomach for the troubadour's art.

A soft tap on her chamber door brought her head up.

'My lady, you are wanted in the count's solar.'

'Wanted?' Leonor wiped her eyes with the sleeve of her tunic. 'For what purpose?'

'I know not, lady,' the young woman replied. 'Save that you should wear a gown...' She flicked her eyes over Leonor's wrinkled tunic. 'And that you should come quickly. The Templar, Reynaud, is there, as well.'

God grant her strength. Surely whatever awaited could be no worse than what had gone before. Her heart ached, but she must move forwards with courage.

With trembling hands she donned a gown of pale blue sendal, the sleeves lined in russet silk, and girdled it with a length of gold chain. Keeping her back straight as a lance, she descended the staircase to the door of her great-uncle's private solar.

Laughter sounded from behind the solid oak panel. Men's laughter. Her heart all but stopped.

The door swung open, and she paused to gather her wits, then advanced into the room with determined steps. Someone thrust a wine goblet into her hand, and without conscious thought she took a sip of the rich liquid.

'You are to be married,' Aunt Alais said softly.

Married! Her heart plummeted. Count Henri had betrothed her to some knight or duke or—she did not care which. Whoever it was, she would never wed him. She belonged to Reynaud. She would never have another man. Never.

Gradually she let her gaze travel to Reynaud, standing against the wall next to Henri. He moved towards her, raised her hand to his lips. Her heart stopped at the look on his face.

His eyes were as she would remember them always; green as the sea, they bored into her own with such intensity her belly contracted.

'Should we send a rider after Benjamin?' he asked quietly. 'He could carry the news to your father in Granada.'

She hesitated, a frown creasing her forehead. 'That we should not.'

'Ah,' Reynaud murmured. 'And why is that?'

'I—I sent one of Alais's pups with Benjamin. Wrapped it in linen and made a soft bed for it behind the saddle. But…he does not yet know of it.'

Reynaud sent her an odd look. 'Benjamin is fond of younglings, and the hound will need a hearth. Why is that such a difficulty?'

'Because I hid the other pup in his saddlepack.'

Reynaud's mouth twisted. 'Life with you, my Lea, will always hold surprises.'

Life with her? Her heart stumbled. The din in the room faded to a low hum in her ear.

He took one step towards her, lifted the wine cup out of her hand and set it on a side table. In silence he drew her outside into the passageway, away from Count Henri and the others.

He turned to her, clasped both her hands in his. 'Marry me,' he said simply.

Her senses swam. Could it really be true? She raised her face to his, met his grave green eyes and felt her pulse quicken. She was afraid to breathe lest she wake up to find it was but a dream she had woven in her desperation.

'How did this come to be?' she whispered.

'Because I love you.' He kissed her, hard, and held her against his chest. 'And you love me.'

Her heart swelled as if it would burst into blossom.

'That,' she murmured, 'I know well.'

For a very long time, neither of them spoke.

The hot amber sunlight washed over two figures outlined against a pale stone wall, a man and a woman, merging them into one.

Afterword

Following their formation in AD 1118, in the aftermath of the First Crusade, the Knights Templar gained the respect of both Christians and Muslims as bankers, negotiators and diplomatic envoys. Following dissolution of the order in 1314 by Philip IV of France, the Templar treasure disappeared. Some say the Order of St John, known as the Knights Hospitallers, held Templar funds in trust on the island of Malta. Others believe a secret treasury had been established at a place called Rennes-le-Château, near Carcassonne in southern France.

No trace of any treasure has ever been found.

Troubadours flourished in the twelfth-century lands of Langue d'Oc, as southern France was known, drawing on the tradition established by Guillaume, Duke of Aquitaine, grandfather of Eleanor of Aquitaine, and the music and poetry of Moorish Spain to the south.

That musical tradition formed the basis of courtly love popularised by Eleanor and her daughter Marie de France.

Bernat de Ventadourn was one of the most gifted troubadours of his time. Women troubadours, called *trobaritz,* were rare, but the author would like to think Leonor of Moyanne might have been one of them.

Turn the page for a sneak preview of
AFTERSHOCK, *a new anthology*
featuring New York Times
bestselling author Sharon Sala.

Available October 2008.

n o c t u r n e

Dramatic and sensual tales
of paranormal romance.

Chapter 1

October
New York City

Nicole Masters was sitting cross-legged on her sofa while a cold autumn rain peppered the windows of her fourth-floor apartment. She was poking at the ice cream in her bowl and trying not to be in a mood.

Six weeks ago, a simple trip to her neighborhood pharmacy had turned into a nightmare. She'd walked into the middle of a robbery. She never even saw the man who shot her in the head and left her for dead. She'd survived, but some of her senses had not. She was dealing with short-term memory loss and a tendency to stagger. Even though she'd been told the problems were most likely temporary, she waged a daily battle with depression.

Her parents had been killed in a car wreck when she was twenty-one. And except for a few friends—

and most recently her boyfriend, Dominic Tucci, who lived in the apartment right above hers, she was alone. Her doctor kept reminding her that she should be grateful to be alive, and on one level she knew he was right. But he wasn't living in her shoes.

If she'd been anywhere else but at that pharmacy when the robbery happened, she wouldn't have died twice on the way to the hospital. Instead of being grateful that she'd survived, she couldn't stop thinking of what she'd lost.

But that wasn't the end of her troubles. On top of everything else, something strange was happening inside her head. She'd begun to hear odd things: sounds, not voices—at least, she didn't think it was voices. It was more like the distant noise of rapids— a rush of wind and water inside her head that, when it came, blocked out everything around her. It didn't happen often, but when it did, it was frightening, and it was driving her crazy.

The blank moments, which is what she called them, even had a rhythm. First there came that sound, then a cold sweat, then panic with no reason. Part of her feared it was the beginning of an emotional breakdown. And part of her feared it wasn't—that it was going to turn out to be a permanent souvenir of her resurrection.

Frustrated with herself and the situation as it stood, she upped the sound on the TV remote. But instead of *Wheel of Fortune,* an announcer broke in with a special bulletin.

"This just in. Police are on the scene of a kidnapping that occurred only hours ago at The Dakota. Molly Dane, the six-year-old daughter of one of Hollywood's blockbuster stars, Lyla Dane, was taken by force from the family apartment. At this time they have yet to receive a ransom demand. The housekeeper was seriously injured during the abduction, and is, at the present time, in surgery. Police are hoping to be able to talk to her once she regains consciousness. In the meantime, we are going now to a press conference with Lyla Dane."

Horrified, Nicole stilled as the cameras went live to where the actress was speaking before a bank of microphones. The shock and terror in Lyla Dane's voice were physically painful to watch. But even though Nicole kept upping the volume, the sound continued to fade.

Just when she was beginning to think something was wrong with her set, the broadcast suddenly switched from the Dane press conference to what appeared to be footage of the kidnapping, beginning with footage from inside the apartment.

When the front door suddenly flew back against the wall and four men rushed in, Nicole gasped. Horrified, she quickly realized that this must have been caught on a security camera inside the Dane apartment.

As Nicole continued to watch, a small Asian woman, who she guessed was the maid, rushed forward in an effort to keep them out. When one of the men hit her in the face with his gun, Nicole moaned. The violence was too reminiscent of what she'd lived through. Sick to her stomach, she fisted her hands against her belly, wishing it was over, but unable to tear her gaze away.

When the maid dropped to the carpet, the same man followed with a vicious kick to the little woman's midsection that lifted her off the floor.

"Oh, my God," Nicole said. When blood began to pool beneath the maid's head, she started to cry.

As the tape played on, the four men split up in different directions. The camera caught one running down a long marble hallway, then disappearing into a room. Moments later he reappeared, carrying a little girl, who Nicole assumed was Molly Dane. The child was wearing a pair of red pants and a white turtleneck sweater, and her hair was partially blocking her abductor's face as he carried her down the hall. She was kicking and screaming in his arms, and when he slapped her, it elicited an agonized scream that brought the other three running. Nicole watched in horror as one of them ran up and put his hand over Molly's face. Seconds later, she went limp.

One moment they were in the foyer, then they were gone.

Nicole jumped to her feet, then staggered drunkenly. The bowl of ice cream she'd absentmindedly placed in her lap shattered at her feet, splattering glass and melting ice cream everywhere.

The picture on the screen abruptly switched from the kidnapping to what Nicole assumed was a rerun of Lyla Dane's plea for her daughter's safe return, but she was numb.

Before she could think what to do next, the doorbell rang. Startled by the unexpected sound, she shakily swiped at the tears and took a step forward. She didn't feel the glass shards piercing her feet until she took the second step. At that point, sharp pains shot through her foot. She gasped, then looked down in confusion. Her legs looked as if she'd been running through mud, and she was standing in broken glass and ice cream, while a thin ribbon of blood seeped out from beneath her toes.

"Oh, no," Nicole mumbled, then stifled a second moan of pain.

The doorbell rang again. She shivered, then clutched her head in confusion.

"Just a minute!" she yelled, then tried to sidestep the rest of the debris as she hobbled to the door.

When she looked through the peephole in the door, she didn't know whether to be relieved or regretful.

It was Dominic, and as usual, she was a mess.

Nicole smiled a little self-consciously as she opened the door to let him in. "I just don't know what's happening to me. I think I'm losing my mind."

"Hey, don't talk about my woman like that."

Nicole rode the surge of delight his words brought. "So I'm still your woman?"

Dominic lowered his head.
Their lips met.
The kiss proceeded.
Slowly.
Thoroughly.

* * * * *

Be sure to look for the
AFTERSHOCK *anthology next month,*
as well as other exciting paranormal stories
from Silhouette Nocturne.
Available in October wherever books are sold.

nocturne™

NEW YORK TIMES BESTSELLING AUTHOR

SHARON SALA

JANIS REAMES HUDSON
DEBRA COWAN

AFTERSHOCK

Three women are brought to the brink of death...
only to discover the aftershock of their trauma has
left them with unexpected and unwelcome gifts of
paranormal powers. Now each woman must learn to
accept her newfound abilities while fighting for life,
love and second chances....

Available October wherever books are sold.

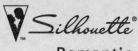

Romantic
SUSPENSE

**Sparked by Danger,
Fueled by Passion.**

USA TODAY bestselling author

Merline Lovelace

Undercover Wife

Secret agent Mike Callahan, code name Hawkeye,
objects when he's paired with sophisticated
Gillian Ridgeway on a dangerous spy mission
to Hong Kong. Gillian has secretly been in love
with him for years, but Hawk is an overprotective
man with a wounded past that threatens to
resurface. Now the two must put their lives—
and hearts—at risk for each other.

Available October wherever books are sold.

REQUEST YOUR FREE BOOKS!

Harlequin® Historical
Historical Romantic Adventure!

2 FREE NOVELS PLUS 2 FREE GIFTS!

YES! Please send me 2 FREE Harlequin® Historical novels and my 2 FREE gifts (gifts are worth about $10). After receiving them, if I don't wish to receive any more books, I can return the shipping statement marked "cancel". If I don't cancel, I will receive 6 brand-new novels every month and be billed just $4.94 per book in the U.S. or $5.49 per book in Canada, plus 25¢ shipping and handling per book and applicable taxes, if any*. That's a savings of 20% off the cover price! I understand that accepting the 2 free books and gifts places me under no obligation to buy anything. I can always return a shipment and cancel at any time. Even if I never buy another book, the two free books and gifts are mine to keep forever.

246 HDN ERUM   349 HDN ERUA

Name	(PLEASE PRINT)	
Address		Apt. #
City	State/Prov.	Zip/Postal Code

Signature (if under 18, a parent or guardian must sign)

Mail to the **Harlequin Reader Service:**
IN U.S.A.: P.O. Box 1867, Buffalo, NY 14240-1867
IN CANADA: P.O. Box 609, Fort Erie, Ontario L2A 5X3

Not valid to current subscribers of Harlequin Historical books.

Want to try two free books from another line?
Call 1-800-873-8635 or visit www.morefreebooks.com.

* Terms and prices subject to change without notice. N.Y. residents add applicable sales tax. Canadian residents will be charged applicable provincial taxes and GST. Offer not valid in Quebec. This offer is limited to one order per household. All orders subject to approval. Credit or debit balances in a customer's account(s) may be offset by any other outstanding balance owed by or to the customer. Please allow 4 to 6 weeks for delivery. Offer available while quantities last.

Your Privacy: Harlequin Books is committed to protecting your privacy. Our Privacy Policy is available online at www.eHarlequin.com or upon request from the Reader Service. From time to time we make our lists of customers available to reputable third parties who may have a product or service of interest to you. If you would prefer we not share your name and address, please check here. ☐

HH08R

MEDITERRANEAN DOCTORS

Demanding, devoted and
drop-dead gorgeous—
These Latin doctors will
make your heart race!

Smolderingly sexy Mediterranean doctors

Saving lives by day…red-hot lovers by night

Harlequin® Historical
Historical Romantic Adventure!

HALLOWE'EN HUSBANDS

With three fantastic stories by

Lisa Plumley
Denise Lynn
Christine Merrill

Don't miss these unforgettable stories about three women who experience the mysterious happenings of Allhallows Eve and come to discover that finding true love on this eerie day is not so scary after all.

Look for
HALLOWE'EN HUSBANDS

Available October
wherever books are sold.

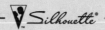

SPECIAL EDITION™

FROM *NEW YORK TIMES* BESTSELLING AUTHOR

LINDA LAEL MILLER

A STONE CREEK CHRISTMAS

Veterinarian Olivia O'Ballivan finds the animals in Stone Creek playing Cupid between her and Tanner Quinn. Even Tanner's daughter, Sophie, is eager to play matchmaker. With everyone conspiring against them and the holiday season fast approaching, Tanner and Olivia may just get everything they want for Christmas after all!

Available December 2008
wherever books are sold.